HIS MAKESHIFT FIANCEE

AWAY TO AFRICA
BOOK TWO

UNOMA NWANKWOR

KEVSTEL PUBLICATIONS

Kevstel Publications

info@kevstel.com

To my beloved mother.
Amama, I was in the middle of this project when the Lord called you home.
Through my devastation and brokenness, your spirit propelled me to THE END.
I miss you like crazy, and I love you. Always & Forever.

AUTHOR'S NOTE

Away to Africa is the second volume of my sweet romance collection, Afro Luv Bites.

Here, we follow the Kalu family. More specifically the three male cousins Arinze, Cheta & Jidenna. His Makeshift Fiancée is Cheta & Reign's story. We first meet the family in New Year's Kiss which is a short prequel. Although you don't have to read that, or book 1(Rent A Bae) to enjoy this, but I'd recommend you do so for maximum enjoyment.

Happy Reading!

In case you are wondering, the first volume, the Billionaire Pact is available on all major online retailers.

PS: The name of the basketball team Cheta plays for has been changed to a fictional one; Atlanta Harriers. A harrier is a hawk like bird. See what I did there...LOL

CHETA KALU

"*A*ppreciate it, man. I didn't think you'd make it."

I dapped my mentor, Jordan Amadu, and allowed him to pull me in for a brotherly hug. "You know I couldn't miss your big five-o." I handed him the gift I brought and surveyed the scene of the enormous backyard.

Burna Boy's "It's Plenty" blared from the huge speakers, and the tables that lined the corners contained an array of food, and there was an open bar with a free flow of drinks. There weren't that many people because Jordan always kept a tight circle, but those that were here ranged from celebs to family. The aroma from the grill drifted through the air, causing me to contemplate the pros and cons of hearing my trainer's mouth if I decided to indulge in a second cheat day.

Wiping the sweat from the bridge of my nose, I adjusted my sunshades and pulled down my ballcap. The scorching July Phoenix sun was nothing to play with—another reason I was thankful I no longer lived in the city. Only for Jordan would I even be out here. The now retired NBA star forward took me under his wing when I was drafted to play for Arizona after college. Being a fellow African playing in the NBA, his guidance and encouragement saw me through the days when I didn't want to deal with all the behind-the-scenes drama that came with being in the league. I'd forever be indebted to him.

I followed Jordan further into the backyard, acknowledging some familiar faces along the way. Despite my efforts at being incognito, I was stopped by some high schoolers for autographs and pictures. Finding a spot to settle in, I was about to ask Jordan about his wife when I looked up and saw her headed in our direction. Rita Amadu always carried herself with an elegance that was almost rare these days. Her petite stature often had people believing she was pampered and a pushover, but that was far from the case. Mess with her husband or children and you'd be shaking in your boots. Meeting her halfway, I greeted her with a kiss on her cheek

"Hi Cheta, I'm so glad you made it. I thought you were still in Nigeria," she said.

"Hey, Mrs. A. Looking good as always. Nah, got back about two weeks ago."

She snaked her arm around Jordan's waist and beamed up at him before returning her focus to me. "Thank you. Have you had anything to eat? Where are you sitting? Can I—"

"Babe, the man just got here. He knows where everything is." Jordan leaned to kiss her temple.

Although I didn't see them as often as I used to, I was no stranger to their Phoenix home. But Rita was only doing what she'd always done—mothered me. She was sweet and not too overbearing, so I allowed it on occasion. Lately, she'd been trying to hook me up with a "good girl." It's like something was in the air because so were my mother and grandmother. My cousin Arinze getting engaged a few months ago now shifted the Kalu matriarch's focus to me.

Love.

I'd been there, done that and wasn't ready for it again, just yet. My primary focus was securing a second championship ring and solidifying my post basketball plans. At thirty-five, I wasn't decided if the upcoming season would be my last season, but I was seriously leaning towards it.

"Nah, I just got here. I see Pops on the grill. I'll go over and say hello."

I chatted with the Amadus a bit more before I made my way to the food and then left to mingle with their new guests. After making light conversation with a few more people, I chopped it up with Jordan's dad before getting a plate of food and something to drink. I didn't plan on staying long since I had to catch an early morning flight back to Atlanta.

I spotted an empty cabana a little ways from the crowd and took my food there to settle in. After a few minutes spent declining requests from some ladies to join me, I was able to start eating. Being in the NBA for over a decade, I could tell by the look of desperation in their eyes and their attire that they were on the prowl for a come up. I wasn't on that kind of time, so I had nothing for them.

While absently watching a game of Marco Polo going on in the pool and scrolling through my social media, I chowed down on the barbequed chicken, coleslaw, and potato salad I had on my plate. I've always enjoyed my own company, so I didn't roll with a lot of people. There wasn't a shortage of people around me, but apart from my cousins Arinze and Jidenna, none of them could say they really knew my moves. I had learned the hard way that not everyone who smiled in your face was your friend. Some of them were the very people that wanted your downfall.

Big Sis Ada: Cheta, please don't forget IK goes camping next week.

I frowned at the text notification that popped up on my phone. I should be used to texts like this by now, but truth be told, I wasn't. Regardless of my feelings, I always came through. My two older sisters were Irish twins and after having them, my mom struggled to conceive again. To hear my sisters tell it, I was the cause of the tension between my parents and them not getting the fatherly love they should've received. A Western education didn't change my father's warped perspective and obsessive want for a male child. What it did was cause a divide between my sisters and me. I wasn't even born yet, and I was being blamed.

As I was growing up, my dad treated me like his prized possession, my mom as her bargaining chip and my sisters as the little brother they tolerated. My sisters' attitudes towards me growing up created a gap between us. One that my money magically had them pressed to close. They both married deadbeats and now expected me to pick up the slack their husbands left. They were my first lesson in the fickleness of humans. I loved them, but I didn't mess with them.

Responding to my sister with a promise to send the money tomorrow, I lifted my drink to my mouth when I felt a shadow cast over me. Jordan took a seat beside me. The look he gave me prepared me for the lecture I knew he was about to give.

"Say what you gotta say, Jay."

He simpered. "So, LST decided to keep you on."

Leaning back in the chair, I twirled my drink and took a sip before meeting his eyes. "Yeah, the test came back in my favor." I shrugged. "Besides, they know I make them a lotta money." LST was one of the elite sports management teams in the country and I had been with them for several years.

"That you do. But you also have to understand that you gotta meet them halfway. You can't be out here reckless. It's getting old."

I waved him off. "Man, half the stuff they be worried about I have no control over. The other half ain't worth talking about."

"Having two women claim you got them pregnant on the same night is worth talking about," he laughed.

"Not when they lying."

"But your reputation does—"

"Jay, man I'm damned if I do, damned if I don't. You know I don't care what people that have no idea who I am, think. I wanna focus on the upcoming season."

He lifted his hand in surrender. I appreciated him looking out, but I wasn't trying to hear it right now. I wanted to relax and face the future. No sense looking back. After almost thirteen years in the league and a wild couple of years, I'd come to terms with the fact that people were always going to think what they wanted to think. Heaven forbid someone could change.

My dad was the middle son of a family of three boys. He and his siblings all studied abroad, married their wives then moved back home to start Kalu International. The company now was worth millions, so I'd never hurt for money. But something about being young and signing a 3.2-million-dollar contract straight outta Morehouse College had me living up to every bad boy athlete stereotype in the book. Especially since it was rare for Morehouse to produce NBA players. Frivolous spending, gambling, or making appearances in the club any chance I got. I was never without a different lady on my arm. My crew rolled deep so sometimes the night ended without incident, other times it didn't.

One thing about me though—I was always ready to do my job. Not to brag, but my game was nice, earning me the nickname Nyce. As long as I won games, brought fans to arenas, and made brands money, my management and the team owners turned a blind eye.

The car accident that nearly took my life put a lot of stuff into perspective. I was traded to Philadelphia then my management company dropped me. Those were the worst years of my life, but I worked my behind off to get my game back to its top-notch state. Then LST came knocking. A few years after I signed with them, they negotiated a deal for me to return to Atlanta to play for the Harriers. I and my cousins were Morehouse Men, so Atlanta was home.

I welcomed the move, and the money made the deal sweeter. I've tried to keep my behind out of the tabloids and be on the straight and narrow, but it was difficult to shake off a reputation that took several years to create. That and the fact that people liked to keep you where they met you.

I'd been doing good though until some chicks popped up last year claiming I was their baby daddy. One moment I'm attending an album release party for one of my rapper homies and the next, I wake up to two women in my hotel room. I still think I was drugged because I couldn't remember anything. I went to empty my bladder and wash my face, and by the time I returned to the room, they were gone. Only to pop up months later talking about I was responsible for both their pregnancies. Thinking about the day I woke up trending on Twitter still gave me chills.

My publicist, Amara Dike, and agent, Marcus Jacobs, gave me an earful and then went to work. A statement was released on my behalf, a gag order was issued, then the waiting began. They'd refused a DNA test until the babies were born. I prayed like I'd never done before and the Big Guy came through, but the damage had been done to the image I'd been trying to clean up.

"Okay, I'mma say this then get off it. You've worked hard in Atlanta. Don't let some foolishness get in the way of where you trying to go."

Nodding, I took another sip. "I hear you, old man. Ain't you supposed to be blowing out some candles?" I lifted my chin.

"I got your old man." He squeezed my shoulder and stood.

I followed suit, smiling as Rita walked behind the caterers, pushing out a three-tier cake. Rita called out for everyone to gather around. As the crowd began to move toward her in the huge tent in the middle of the yard, I felt a presence walk up to us. Recognizing who it was, my jaw clenched immediately.

Vance Henderson.

"Easy, Nyce. Easy," I heard Jordan caution as he eased his way between me and my former best friend turned mortal enemy.

This was the first time I'd seen him in person since our fallout years ago. I shoved my fisted hands into my khaki shorts. Everything I promised myself I'd do to him if I ever saw him again came flooding to the front of my mind.

Vance's eyes danced between me and Jordan. He for sure didn't expect to see me here. "Hey Jay, happy birthday, man. Sorry, I'm late. Finley was—"

"Baby, it's time," Rita's voice cut through the tension.

Perfect timing since I didn't want to hear anything about the woman I'd foolishly thought I could build with.

"Thanks, man, glad you could make it. Here I come, babe." Jordan's eyes warned me against any evil thing I wanted to say or do.

Some days, Vance and Finley's betrayal was a distant memory. Other days, I questioned my judgment for trusting them completely. Majority of the time though, I thanked God for protecting me from what I didn't see coming.

"C, can we—"

"Nah man, save it," I responded and followed Jordan to where the cake was. One thing I didn't do was fake. There was nothing he could say to me that would excuse what he had done. Besides, there was no point. What was done was done. That was in the past.

"Papa, I want the finishing to be perfect. The way they had the doors the last time was tacky."

"Okay, my son. I'll be there myself to make sure it's correct."

At least once a week, my dad and I talked. It was a little after eight p.m. in Phoenix, which made it about four a.m. in Enugu. Chima Kalu had always been an early riser, so I was used to him calling me when he got up in the wee hours of the morning to prepare for morning Mass. Unlike my mom who was more in tune with my schedule and the time difference, my dad called whenever it was convenient for *him*.

True to his nature, Jordan tried to get Vance and me to talk, but that was a hard no for me. Shortly after the cutting of the cake, I said my goodbyes and left. Getting back to my suite, I got my fit together for my early morning flight, took a quick shower, and settled in for the night. While I searched for something to occupy my mind, my phone rang.

I was building a vocational school in my hometown and my dad was overseeing the project. I attended high school back in Enugu and I hung around some very smart guys. Their families didn't have the resources to further their education, leaving them idle and frustrated. This led to some of them doing the wrong things to earn money.

While the Kalu foundation sponsored qualifying students through four years of university education, I wanted to offer another solution in the form of a trade school. I was sparing no expense, so I wanted it done right. I needed it to compare to any international standard. We broke ground late last year and things were moving along nicely.

"You say you're not home. When do you go back to Atlanta? How are Arinze and his American wife?"

I chuckled. "I head back in the morning. You do know they're not married yet, papa."

"*Ehn*, but it's coming, so she's already our wife."

One thing my dad was good for was a debate. Since I wasn't ready to engage him now, I agreed with his logic and moved the discussion to other things. Several minutes later, he reminded me for maybe the millionth time that he was being conferred a chieftaincy title in six weeks, so I had to be by his side. Then he started his closing act. Like clockwork, at the end of our conversations, he retold the story of how he and his brothers looked out for each other when they were in "the abroad." So, I and my cousins should do the same.

Then he proceeded to ask when I talked to my sisters last. I could tell that over the years, he blamed himself for the state of our relationship, but I couldn't do anything about that. So, I gave the same generic answer, "just the other day." Then he ended with praying over me. After we disconnected, I placed my hands behind my head and mentally went over what the following day meant for me.

During the off-season, I co-anchored sports sections for different networks. Last year was the first time I anchored for ESPN. According to Marcus, they liked me so much that they were thinking of offering me my own show. The thing with the two women paused those talks. Amara kept them from taking the offer entirely off the table. Having my show on ESPN was a dream come true. This week, I'd get the chance to meet with the network executives and remind them I was worth the chance. Saying a quick prayer, I set the alarm on my phone and was about to set it on the nightstand when it buzzed. A grin crept up my face at the text.

Reign: Since you won't stop, I guess I should thank you. Ps: This doesn't make us friends.

I laughed out loud and responded.

It only took two months but at last, you've found your manners

Reign: Now will you stop sending them?

Not a chance

She replied with an emoji of a hand across the face, and I responded with a laughing emoji.

Reign Davis was the owner of a skincare line and store located in the same complex where Arinze's fiancée, Jasmine's flower shop was located. I saw her even before Jasmine became a part of the family. The minute I laid eyes on her, I wanted her. In what capacity I didn't know, but that was decided for me when my reputation preceded me. Shawty wouldn't even give me the time of day.

The last time I saw her was two months ago. I'd pulled up to see Jasmine at her shop when I saw Reign in her car, crying. Something about seeing the normally confident, feisty, and assertive woman in tears pierced my heart. The favor of God was on me that day because she allowed me to comfort her. Even told me the reason for her tears.

She'd returned from visiting her grandmother, who had Alzheimer's, in a nursing home. It was something she did twice a month on Saturdays. Ever since then, I opened a tab with Jasmine and had flowers sent to Reign to cheer her up. After several "you don't have to do this" and "stop" in all caps texts, this was the first time I got more than a phrase from her. I needed to pull up on her. I might be breaking down those sky-high walls.

2

***

REIGN DAVIS

*M*y eyes darted toward the timer on my left for a quick gauge of how long I had left. Deciding I could get two more questions in, I faced the camera.

"I'm gonna take this last pre-submitted question, then I'm gonna take one from the comments."

Every Tuesday, I went live on my Instagram, answering skincare questions from my followers. When time permitted, I also gave them a sneak peek of the stuff I had coming up. Self-care with emphasis on skincare was something I was passionate about. Hence the birth of my baby, Body Glow Essentials, six years ago. My skincare products weren't made from recipes I got online and tweaked to my liking. Nothing wrong with that if that was your thing, but this wasn't that. After my business degree, I obtained a master's in chemistry, got my certification as a cosmetologist, and worked with a few dermatologists to craft the perfect products for natural skin care.

"There's no hard rule on how many times you should exfoliate. It depends on how powerful the ingredients are. The Body Glow Peel Pads can be used twice a week, which is the general rule. Okay, last question, let me see." I squinted to look through the comments. "Good question @anada45, the five basics of a good skincare routine are cleanse, tone, treat, target and, moisturize. If you do that, I promise, you can't go wrong.

"All right y'all, I gotta go, but don't forget to like, share, and subscribe to our YouTube channel. I should have a tutorial up by the weekend. Love you, BGEFam. Check out the website. The grape and brown sugar body scrub is back in stock. See y'all same time next week. Remember, your body is the Lord's temple; you gotta treat it right."

The LIVE ended and I leaned back in my chair and took a deep breath. I was trying to be more consistent with these live Q&A's, so I made a point to do them once I got in my office. Before I could do anything else, I needed some caffeine. I scooted my chair back, stood and smoothed down my dress and made my way to the door. The store didn't open until nine a.m., so I still had some time to walk a couple of doors down to the coffee shop to get a Thai cold coffee.

As I walked to the front of the store, the door chimed, and in walked Ebonie Smith, my business partner. She had a day job as a marketer, so only made it in once or twice a week. Since her job required a lot of travel, she worked mostly remotely on the business part of things. Sourcing opportunities and deals to create awareness for BGE was her forte. I hadn't expected her this early, but considering what she had in her hand, I knew it was the Lord's doing.

A smile crept up my lips and with hurried strides, I approached her and removed the cup holder in her hand. My Thai cold coffee sat pretty with a cup of hot coffee.

"Well, good morning to you too then," she said.

"If you had waited, I would've said good morning *and* thanked you for my coffee." I playfully rolled my eyes.

Ebonie giggled. "I don't know who told you it was yours, but go off then." Turning to lock the door, she paused. "I see Lula getting out of her car. I didn't know she was coming this morning."

Lula was our part-time salesclerk. She worked Thursdays to Saturdays, which were the days I designated for being in the studio mixing and researching enhancements for our products. I also did inventory, restocking and shipping large orders on those days. The rest of the time, I could handle the incoming traffic between meetings and other daily tasks.

"Yeah, I got behind on some of the mixes for the serum and facial cream, so I'm gonna be in the studio a lot today."

After waiting for Lula to enter and exchanging greetings, Ebonie and I made our way to the back of the store. When doing business out of my living room became nearly impossible, I began searching for space. I wanted a retail store, but I also wanted somewhere I could have an office, a studio space, and a warehouse all in one. After weeks of searching, I found the perfect location in Asili Plaza. Most days, I spent more time here than I did in my townhome, so I was glad it suited my needs perfectly. From my days on Esty to where I was now, I knew it was only God's favor.

When business started to pick up and became too over-whelming, I reached out to Ebonie. We met in college and main-tained contact over the years. She believed in my vision right from the beginning. She told me that when I decided to stop being scared and do it, I should let her know. After working for L'Oréal for two years, I decided it was time. So, I did. She was happy to invest in the business and become my partner. I was the majority owner, but I wouldn't have minded an equal split. Her input has been invaluable, and I was blessed to have her.

"Girl, I see you," Ebonie said, entering my office.

Walking behind my desk, I took a sip of my coffee before setting it down. "What are you talking about?"

Ebonie plopped down on the small, turquoise couch and

pulled the coffee table closer to her. "Don't play. I see your man sent you flowers again."

I turned to the sample product display cabinet in the corner and shrugged. On top of it sat the fuchsia ginger jar that contained pink roses and white daisies with fresh greenery. They were so beautiful. If only they were from someone else.

"Don't start—"

"I don't know what you're tripping for. If an NBA player, not just any player—we're talking about Nyce, point guard for the Harriers, wanted to send me flowers, have lunch delivered to me, and cared about my wellbeing, why would I refuse?"

Cheta "Nyce" Kalu was the current thorn in my side. I hadn't seen him in several weeks, but he made sure I didn't forget he was near. That man was fine, fine. Something that must run in the family genes considering his two cousins were equally as handsome. Google said he stood at 6'3, but it said nothing about his piercing brown eyes, well-toned frame, and deep waves he kept in a mean fade. He was every woman's dream because they stayed fighting over him.

I had too much to lose to take his flirtatious behavior seriously. The last time I saw him in all his melanated glory, every nerve ending in my body begged me to live on the wild side, but that was never gonna happen.

Sitting at my desk, I shook the mouse to wake my device up before meeting the heat of Ebonie's stare. "First, I didn't ask him to. Second, I have no desire to be the current center of attraction of a man whore. I got enough going on as it is."

"I don't see you turning away his attention either. You eat every lunch and keep every bouquet."

My brows furrowed. "Why would I waste good food? Especially coming from the best dining Atlanta has to offer. I asked Jas to get her kinfolk to stop with the flowers, but she says I gotta take that up with him."

I rolled my eyes remembering the conversation I had with

Jasmine Bowman, the owner of Luxe Petals. That's where the flowers were from. She was also the fiancée of Cheta's cousin, Arinze. The way she laughed at my frustration almost made me want to push her down for being an accomplice.

Ebonie laughed at my rant. I don't know why everyone thought it was funny. I was far from ungrateful, but more than anything, I wanted him to forget about me. Our meeting last year was so random. I'd be a liar if I denied the attraction between us. Then he opened his mouth and his arrogance seeped out. Sexy though he may be, he grated my nerves. That night, I did a Google search. Although he did deserve his bragging rights on the court, his reputation was a mess. I'd been on the run from him ever since.

"All I'm saying is, the man is asking for one date. What can it hurt? He finds out you stay late in the shop and sends you food. He found out about your grandma and sends flowers to make sure you feel better. I mean—"

"Since you and Jas are founders of his fan club, you'd be happy to know that for this bouquet, I sent him a thank you text."

Over the last few months, I found out that if for nothing else, Cheta was caring. A trait I discovered was reserved for only a few. As flattered as I was, I knew he was more trouble than I could deal with.

"Hmmm, a real thank you or a thank you with sass? I know you, Rei." Ebonie pulled out her iPad.

"At least, it's progress. Can we move on to the agenda for the day?" I opened my project management tool.

Ebonie raised her hands in surrender. "You got it. I know you got trust issues, but sometimes you gotta take that leap."

"Thanks, Oprah. So, what we got?"

"Good news. Remember that hospitality conference we attended last month? I got an email from Coleman and they're moving BGE to the second phase of the process."

My hands shot up and I let out a squeal of excitement. "Eb, I should slap you. Instead of leading with that, we over here talking about stuff that don't matter."

Ebonie giggled. "How are you only 5'2", but always threatening bodily harm on folks? Girl, simmer down, let me tell you the details and requirements."

Taking another sip of my beverage, I lifted my brow. "My height has nothing to do with these hands. So, what's up?"

Over the next hour, Ebonie and I went over the email that Coleman Hospitality Group sent over. Our products included scrubs, body butters, cleansers, toners, exfoliating peel pads, serums, soaps, lotions, and creams. We currently had two major lines and some specialty products. Most of our current sales came from our online store. The normal logical next step would be to get our products into bigger name retail stores. But I wanted to head in another direction.

For the past eighteen months, I'd been working on an exclusive spa line that hadn't been launched to the public. Lush by BGE included a cleanser, scrub, hydrating lotion, moisturizer, bath salt and massage oil. My goal was to supply Lush by BGE to the spas of boutique hotels in wholesale quantities. When a hotel guest decided to get the spa treatment, I wanted our products to be what they used. A few months ago, there was a large trade show hosted at the World Congress Center and I took samples and pitched to several hotels. The focus of the show was Black-owned, small businesses that had been in business for only five to eight years.

Coleman was my dream client–faith-based, family-focused with superb customer service. Monica Coleman-Hunt, the CEO, was a Black woman who was all about business. She seemed to have it all. A gorgeous family and a thriving business she inherited from her grandfather and took to greater heights. I hadn't had the pleasure of meeting her, but she was one of my business role models. At last count, Coleman had one hundred and fifty hotels across the nation and two in Canada.

Their pitch slots filled up fast, but I was on the waiting list. I prayed, cried, fasted, and perfected my pitch in case I got a chance with them. My God was working because right there at the trade show, after pitching to four other hotel and resort chains, I got a notification on my phone that a slot with Coleman had become available for me. I'd been knocked down so much in life that I had to take this moment in.

"I can't believe this. I mean I know it's not—"

"Nope. Stop there because I know you're about to use your mouth to cancel this blessing. You've worked hard for the last seven years to get where you are. You deserve this, Reign."

"Yeah, you're right. Let me stop."

"Thank you! Okay, so I will get all the paperwork together. Info for financials, our business proposal and stuff. You work on solidifying the recipe and all the creative things you do so well. They said their CEO might be present when we meet with them in two weeks." Ebonie swiped through her iPad, probably making sure she wasn't forgetting anything.

My mind was racing. Since the tradeshow, I'd wanted to change the container designs, tweak the logo, and add a new herb and root I'd recently discovered during my research. It would make my products richer in antioxidants and vitamins. It wouldn't change the fragrance, but enhance it.

"Did you hear back from Coup de Main?" I asked. My regular virtual assistant was on maternity leave, so we'd sourced a temporary replacement from one of the top-notch agencies in Atlanta.

"Yeah, that's my next meeting. Once I ensure she meets our needs, I'll send her over to you." Ebonie stood.

"Where are you going?"

"Ummm... my mama is in Montgomery but since you nosey... home. I have some maintenance people coming to fix my garage door. Also, I need to run some errands before my hot date tonight. We can't all be like you."

"I'm not touching that one."

"'Cause you know it's the truth." She hung her bag over her shoulder and headed for the door. "I'll be outta town the rest of the week for the nine-to-five, but call me if you need me."

"Thanks, Eb, I don't know what I'd do without you."

"And I you, but we'll never have to find out." She winked. "I know you're headed home this weekend. Please try and enjoy yourself." She opened the door and left, but not before yelling over her shoulder. "You got this."

I leaned back in my chair and groaned. Home was Savannah, Georgia where my parents lived. I loved the town I grew up in, not being one of those who wanted to leave home and never return. However, I couldn't forget that most of my memories weren't good ones either. I tried to make the three-hour trip home every month to check on my parents. This time though, I was glad I wouldn't be the sole focus of the town's gossips, aka church mothers. My younger siblings were also flying down on summons from Claudine and Lamont Davis.

My dad had fully recovered from a recent stroke and my mom was throwing a celebratory gathering to celebrate. My sister, Deja, was a corporate trainer for a telecom company and currently lived in Madrid, while my brother, Dominic, lived in California, working in tech in Silicon Valley. My siblings and I were close, but I wished for once they'd stop pretending that my parents didn't treat them like golden geese while treating me like the biggest disappointment of their existence.

Even though I was two years older, I've lived under Deja's shadow for as long as I could remember. Our personalities were worlds apart. Deja was beautiful by all conventional and unconventional standards. Long natural hair, brown eyes, glowing dark chocolate skin, long legs giving her the perfect height. She ran track and was very popular in school.

I on the other hand... well let's just say, I didn't even have an identity of my own. I was known as Deja's sister. Suffering from acne and hating most things about my appearance made me very insecure. However, my insecurities and the mistakes I made because of them had nothing to do with my sister. That was all me. We loved each other very much, but after all these years, I wished for once, she'd look at things with our parents from my perspective instead of the rose-colored glasses she preferred to adorn. I shook my head to rid myself of the bad mood that was about to take over my day.

I had accomplished a lot for myself. Even if my parents couldn't let one mistake, although costly, go. I was proud of what I'd accomplished.

It was time to get back to work. I picked up my drink and twirled it around while jotting down some notes. If this deal went through, I'd finally be able to give them what had their panties in a bunch for years and be free.

"I wish you and Ma would put the claws away for once," Deja said.

"And I wish you'd call a spade a spade. But we can't always have what we want, now can we?" I pushed the cart down another aisle, looking for the specific brand of allspice my mother had to have.

At thirty-three, I would think my mother would recognize that just because she gave me life didn't mean she could continue to throw shade and I wouldn't say anything back. I'd been back home barely six hours and already, I couldn't wait to leave. My sister had arrived the day before and Dominic would be arriving later tonight. It had been a rough week and I was tired. Deja and I were still catching up when my mom complained of not having allspice. I offered to go to the store and get it, but of course, nothing I did was good enough for her.

"Rei, Ma was trying to say you didn't get the right one."

"But that ain't what she said, is it?" I rolled my eyes at my sister and bent to pick up the correct brand. "She didn't need to start fussing about how as long as I've lived at home, I should've known the brand." I threw the spice in the basket and walked toward the juice aisle. "So, I moved back home after college. Does she always have to remind me of their expectations I didn't meet?"

Deja flung her arms around my neck, forcing me into a hug. "You're right. You know she likes to bait you. Don't fall for it… pleeeeaaaase. I'm back in town for the next few weeks. I want to enjoy my family."

"Get off me Dee, that whiny voice no longer works." I giggled because she knew like I did that once she used her fake baby voice, I'd do anything for her.

"Please, for me."

"Okay, dang. Get off me so we can get this stuff and leave." I picked up a bottle of strawberry lemonade and placed it in the cart. We walked around getting some more items while Deja filled me in on the new man she was seeing and her life in Madrid. I'd heard about most of it on the phone, but the excitement in her eyes told me she was really happy, and I couldn't be prouder of my sister. As we headed to check out, I prayed the next two days would fly by.

And fly by it did. Two days later, my brother carried my bag to my car while I waited for my dad to get off the phone. My mother was in the kitchen packing leftovers for me. The weekend wasn't as bad as I thought it would be. After the rough patch we had when I first arrived, my mother and I decided to call a truce. I guess the fact she had her other kids here and Deja working extra hard to run interference had something to do with it.

My dad moved around pretty well, and I was thankful he was still among the living. The cookout was amazing. Friends and family came out to celebrate with us. Food and drinks were in abundance. Music blasted and general good vibes flowed through the atmosphere. I had spent the earlier part of the day dodging questions about the state of my personal life.

Once the party started to wind down, my siblings and I and some of Dominic's friends tidied up. The professional cleaning crew would arrive in the morning, but my childhood home looked somewhat decent. Now it was time for me to return to base. The next several days were going to be packed with work before I headed to New York for the biggest meeting of my career.

"I packed you some mac and cheese, yams, and potato salad. There's some barbeque chicken and ribs in the other container. Lord knows you need to eat more." My mother handed the cooler to Dominic to take to the car.

Ignoring that last remark, I said. "Thanks, Ma."

My dad appeared from his den. "You ready to hit the road?"

"Yes, Dad. I was waiting on you to get off the phone."

He pulled me into a hug and kissed my cheek. "So, when are you going to New York?"

"Week after next."

He nodded, but didn't say *the* words. The words I desperately needed and wanted to hear from him. From both my parents. That they were proud of me. When I shared the news of my new project with them, they seemed happy, but not satisfied. Over the years, it was something I'd become used to, but it still didn't feel good. After a few more words of advice from them, I said my goodbyes, and my brother walked me outside.

"You know they love you right?" Dominic said.

"They sure have a funny way of showing it, Nic."

"Well, I love you and I'm proud of you, big sis, for real. You never let words or perception knock you off your game. I respect and admire that."

I willed back my tears and buried my face in my brother's chest. "I love you too, Nic." I took a step back, and climbed into my car. "Tell Dee, I couldn't wait any longer, but I'll be expecting her in two days. You have a safe trip back and call me when you land."

Dominic nodded and gave me a two-finger salute. He closed my door, and I started the engine. It was time to leave all the stuff I had no control over behind and focus on what I could control.

3

CHETA

Taking the back entrance into the Mercedes Benz Stadium, I adjusted my ball cap and checked the time on my phone. I made good time in spite of the impromptu call from my mother. God knows I loved that woman, but she was forever trying to use me to get something from my dad.

"You know he listens to you."

That was always her line. I understood how these things worked, but sometimes I wanted no parts of it. She was his wife. Who should better know how to get whatever she needed from him? The subtle manipulation by her and my sisters was the reason I found it hard to take people, especially women, at face value. I did a lot of work to let go of my mistrust of women, then Finley happened.

I shook my head to mentally escape the rabbit hole I was about to go down. I sent Arinze a text asking for their ETA. It was Saturday afternoon and some of my teammates and I were participating in the annual Family and Friends Summer Back to School drive. It was an event hosted by the franchise in partnership with the community. The event was supposed to normalize us as everyday people by us having our families here. Leaders of the community and politicians also came through. Generally, we had a good time—packing up school supplies for kids, doing a mini-exhibition, drills, and providing refreshments for everyone.

For me though, these things were a mixed bag. As the face of the team, I had to pose and take pictures with people I couldn't stand. These politicians were the same people that made the laws that forced families that would otherwise be comfortable to have to depend on things like this.

I wasn't opposed to charity as I had a few of them myself. I knew that in society, it was always the work of those who had more to reach down and lift others. It was the publicity of it all that got on my nerves. Couldn't we just do the stuff in private and keep it moving? I knew it was part of the job, but I didn't have to like it.

For this event, the governor-elect was joining us, and I was looking forward to meeting the Black woman that'd been shaking tables. Ms. Tracy Dickerson's record spoke for itself. Right from her days as a State Representative, she backed up everything she said with action. Of course, I didn't agree with every item on her agenda, but anything was better than the dude that had the office now.

As I entered the facility, they had music coming from the DJ booth, and the caterers were set up in the corner. My phone buzzed and I looked down to see Arinze reply that they'd be here within the hour. I responded with a thumbs up, pocketed my phone and walked over to Coach Reynolds in the corner.

As I approached, Zane walked up to me. He was our team's center. He was sick on the defense and the one person I would consider a friend. For the most part, I got along with everyone. My position required it. It also helped that no one got on my nerves too much. But Zane was my boy. He and I arrived in Atlanta to play for the Harriers at the same time and we'd clicked ever since.

"Hey man, what's good?" I asked, as he and I slapped hands and drew each other in for a brotherly hug.

"Chilling, man. When you get back?" he asked.

"Couple of weeks ago."

He and I chatted a little bit, catching up on what'd been going on since the season ended. His mama and younger brother were already here with him. For the past couple of years, none of my family had been able to attend with me because of our schedules. Arinze, an actor and movie consultant, traveled a lot. Although since he got engaged, he'd been trying to get it under control.

Jidenna, a sculptor, also traveled frequently, although not as much as Arinze. Nowadays, he turned down way more gigs than he used to. I didn't blame him though. He was a widowed single father, and my niece, Uju, was his heart and he tried to give her as much stability as possible.

As we talked, some other members of the team joined us until Coach came over.

"Hey guys," he spoke.

We all returned his greeting. When I first got here, he and I bumped heads a lot. He judged me based on what he'd heard, and I wasn't taking the shady shots he tried to throw my way. It took the intervention of the team owners for us to get on the same page. Ever since then, we'd been cool. I wasn't above being taught, but you weren't going to disrespect me either.

"Okay guys, you know the drill. The coordinator will be over in a minute to brief you on your positions." He looked over at me and continued, "Nyce, there's been a slight change in plans. Ms. Dickerson's team has requested that you do the interview with her when she arrives."

I looked over at the media booth. I knew they were here, but I had intentionally avoided even looking that way. I knew I'd have to talk to them, but my teammates would be with me, and I always tried to defer most questions to them. One could say that my years of being chastised by the media had given me an aversion to them.

Years ago, I'd stopped granting any exclusives or responding to any of the sensational stories they wrote. Maturity helped me figure out that when I was silent, they had nothing to quote. If it wasn't team business or didn't have anything to do with my sponsorships and/or endorsements, the media got nothing outta me. I thought that would get them off my back. But it only fueled whatever obsession they had going on. My publicist and I disagreed on responding most of the time. But I let her have her way as long as the response was generic.

"Coach, come on man." I glanced at the media booth.

My brows dipped some more when I made eye contact with Simone Baxter from *ATL Sports Today*. On the outside, Simone was a very beautiful woman, but I had firsthand knowledge of her ugly attitude. She was supposed to be a respectable journalist, but I was sure she fed information to the blogs. When she first started interviewing me, I swear it felt personal. Zane thought I was tripping until we found out that she was the cousin of someone I went on a couple of dates with in the past. I had no control over the stories these women told themselves after a few dates, but I knew for a fact I was very clear on where I stood.

"I know, but I was told it'll take about fifteen minutes, tops. The governor-elect has other business to attend to, so she won't be here when we normally do the interviews." Coach patted me on the back.

Zane held his fist to his mouth trying to stifle his laughter. Before I could lay into him, we heard commotion at the entrance. The governor-elect and her team walked in. I strolled over with Coach, and the introductions were made. After that, we made our way to the side of the booth where Simone and her team were set up. While Ms. Dickerson took a quick phone call, I was being mic'ed up. Simone strode over and I acknowledged her with a nod.

"So, you can't speak now?" she sassed.

I deadpanned her and she smirked. This wasn't our first rodeo. I knew she had some irrelevant questions she was going to sneak into the interview, but hopefully, with the governor-elect here, she'd reign herself in. A few minutes later, as the interview was about to commence, I spotted my family walking in. I smiled when I saw Jidenna stop my niece from running over to me.

"Welcome to a special edition of *ATL Sports Today*," Simone started when the cameras started rolling. "We're at the Harriers annual Family and Friends Summer Back to School event. Today we get to sit down with the governor-elect of Georgia, Tracy Dickerson and none other than Atlanta's favorite Harrier, Cheta "Nyce" Kalu."

I smiled as I could see it pained her to say those words. For the next few minutes, she explained to her audience the meaning and significance of the day's event. I chimed in to fill in the gaps where I could. Next, she turned to the governor-elect and asked her some political questions and what the events like these meant to her and the state. The more we talked, my reservations melted away. Maybe Simone could be civil in mixed company. When I heard the next question out of her mouth, I realized I spoke too soon.

"Cheta, you just successfully renegotiated your contract. Will the city finally get the championship we've been waiting on, or is it money wasted?"

I felt Ms. Dickerson's eyes on me and my chest burned with rage. I struggled to keep my teeth and hands from clenching. My contract negotiations were no secret. A pay raise was expected, although it wasn't supposed to be common knowledge yet. Since I came to Atlanta, we'd won every eastern conference final except the last one. However, the issues surrounding the actual championship had a lot of layers and nuances to it. Something she'd reported on herself. Her bringing it up now was spiteful and foul. I'd been doing this for a while, so I refused to play her game.

Plastering on a smile, I snickered. "Lemme get back to you on that. Today is all about the kids and this wonderful event I'm glad to be a part of."

Simone smiled, then gave her closing remarks. A few minutes later, we were done. Quickly removing the mic, I stepped outside of the booth and waited for the governor-elect. With all the women in my family, I knew never to disrespect a woman, but one of these days, I'd be sure to give Simone exactly what she was looking for.

Soon after, Ms. Dickerson exited the booth, and we walked over to a large table where all the supplies were set up. Surrounded by the team, she gave her opening remarks and the event officially kicked off.

A few hours later, all the major work had been done. We'd packed over two thousand backpacks, played games with the kids, watched an exhibit game and now it was time to eat. We fixed our plates and found an empty tent to settle in. My niece was by my side. After cutting her hamburger into halves, I positioned her iPad in front of her, then I turned to Jasmine.

"Jazzy Jas, why you ain't come with your girl?" I asked, referring to her by the nickname I'd given her.

The way she and my cousin got together had me hella suspicious but seeing their love and how happy my cousin was, she was all right with me. I couldn't stand their overly PDA behinds sometimes, but it was all love over here.

"CK, the last time you sent me to Reign, she almost bit my head off. No sir, you're going to have to do your own legwork."

I chuckled. For someone so little, Reign was mean as heck. "I be trying man, but she won't give me no play."

"Then maybe you need to move on," Arinze chimed in.

"Nze, if you can't be part of the solution, don't add to the problem."

"Do you really like her, or is it the chase for you?" Jidenna asked.

I raised my hands in exasperation. "That's what I'm trying to find out! I'm intrigued and *I dey feel am, but anything else I no know*. She won't let me."

The last time I heard from Reign was a couple of weeks ago when I was in Phoenix. When I returned, I was informed that ESPN had to move our meeting, so I fulfilled some other obligations I had. Between other meetings and a brand photoshoot, I only had time for one pop up. She wasn't there that day and I got caught up in other stuff I had to handle, so I hadn't had the time to go looking for her again. I was brought out of my head when my niece tapped my arm.

"Uncle Cheta, it's not playing anymore." She frowned and I couldn't help but smile.

"Wassup, JuJu?"

"The internet is not connecting." She pointed to her device.

"A'ight hold on, let me connect you to my hotspot."

"She shouldn't be on that thing anyway. It's family time," her father said.

I cut my eyes at him. Uju's mother died during childbirth, so I and Arinze played a huge role in helping Jidenna raise her. We spoiled her, and truth be told, she had us wrapped around her little finger. We tried to stay on the same page with what she was allowed to do, but recently, Jidenna was stricter with her. I knew his change had to do with his mom and our grandmother, something I was going to get with him about.

"*Hapụ ya*," I spoke in Igbo telling Jidenna to leave it alone.

He started to argue when I felt a presence approaching us. I raised my head and grunted as I saw Simone sauntering her way over here. The whole team had sat down with her for a follow-up interview, but I remained silent the whole time, nodding, smiling, and throwing the questions to my teammates.

Arinze followed the direction of my gaze, then turned back to me. "Behave. You know she has an agenda." Right after my first interview with her, I filled them in on her games.

She stopped at our table and there was an awkward silence. I didn't want my niece to see me act out, so I maintained my cool.

"Hey Cheta, you have a lovely family. Aren't you going to introduce me?" she asked.

"Simone, move around," I growled.

"There's no need to be rude."

"And there's no need for you to be here. Yet, here you are."

Ignoring me, she went ahead and introduced herself. Then she honed in on Arinze, and in my peripheral, I caught Jasmine straightening her back. I smirked. After telling Arinze she loved his movies, which was probably a lie, she tried to make small talk with a very disinterested Uju. I knew she wanted me to say something that she'd twist, but I maintained. Arinze saw me slipping though, and he stood and helped Jasmine up. It was time to go. Arinze and Jasmine were headed to Paris later tonight. He was shooting a new movie and she was going to spend a week with him before returning home. The rest of us stood and after an awkward goodbye, Simone continued on her way.

"One of these days…one of these days," I seethed.

"Since we don't put our hands on women, nothing's going to happen. You'll avoid her until she gets tired," Arinze said.

"Say the word CK and I got you," Jasmine said.

Arinze narrowed his eyes at her. "No, you don't."

"Appreciate it Jazzy Jas, but you know Nze's a hater. Also, I can't have you fighting."

She kissed Arinze's lips. "I don't have to lift a finger to cut her down to size."

"Yeah, but she ain't worth it," Jidenna added.

We packed up our trash and moved over to the large bin to discard it. Jidenna was right. If Simone was worth the trouble, my partner in crime and cousin, Ifunanya, would be here in a heartbeat. FiFi, as I called her, was Arinze's second younger sister and she and I were tight. The family called us five and six. I made a mental note to check on her.

As we all walked out of the building, I reminded my cousins that I'd be in New York by mid-week for the ESPN meeting. Getting to the parking garage, we said our goodbyes and I got in my black Porsche Panamera headed for home. After the day I had, I needed a shower and a few episodes of *All American* before I took myself to bed.

For the last hour and some change, I'd been in this large conference room with Marcus and the two dudes from ESPN. I'd given my spiel on what I hoped to add to the channel, then answered some questions they had. This opportunity with the channel would be dope and I was excited. Satisfaction settled in my stomach as part of my retirement plan was coming together. The possibilities were endless, especially with the news I'd received right before I walked in.

While Marcus and the men talked specifics, I half listened while I scrolled through my phone. I was very much involved in everything concerning my career, so I would be combing over the documents before I signed anything. For right now though, I'd let Marcus do what he got a commission for. Besides, I trusted him.

As usual, when I went to Instagram, I found myself on Reign's page. My heart did the weird thing it did when I stared at her pictures for too long. I wasn't a stalker by any means, but I was really intrigued by her. She knew who I was and could care less. I knew that was a played-out stereotype. But I don't care what nobody said, when you have women willing to do anything for you because you are a professional ball player, someone who wasn't moved by it was always refreshing. Reign dodged me like I used to duck those bill collectors in college. Not that I didn't have money to pay, but I somehow always waited till the last minute.

She posted a picture about an hour ago. She looked good in

the burgundy crop top she had on. A part of me was ignited with desire while another part of me twinged with jealousy at the exposed part of her flawless, golden-brown skin. I knew it was a ridiculous emotion to have, but what could I say?

Reign let her long ginger locs hang down, framing her oval face. Those jeans she had on hugged her body effortlessly. Her caption read "Jesus take the wheel, NYC bound." What were the odds? I wanted to comment on her picture, but I didn't want to bring any unnecessary attention her way.

Already, I had read two blog posts about me from *Tatafo Tales* and the other from *The Shade Space*. They were the two blogs that kept my name on their page. For petty, simple stuff too. I got it, I was clickbait, but they needed to find some other business. *Tatafo* was at least decent. *The Shade Space* was the worst, and I knew they got some of their information from Simone freaking Baxter.

I clicked over to my messages and sent Reign a text instead, smiling at the last one she left on read.

I see you heading to NYC

"Cheta, you good?" Marcus asked.

I pocketed my phone and turned to him. "I'm cool."

"Okay, so we'll go back with the counter numbers Marcus asked for. If everything stays the same between now and when we get back to you, I don't see a problem," one of the executives said.

I knew that was code for "as long as there isn't a new scandal with your name on it." Since that's what stalled the talks the last time. Even though it was proven that I wasn't guilty of what I was accused of, the damage was done. After giving time frames and next step expectations, we all stood and shook hands. Marcus and I hung back while the gentlemen left.

Leaning back in my chair, I turned to face him. "You think they'll go for those numbers?"

He furrowed his brows. "Don't you trust me?"

Grinning, I countered, "That don't have nothing to do with my money or potential loss of it."

"Man, we good. Everyone's on their inclusivity train and although ESPN has a good number of Black anchors already, having one that is Nigerian-American is huge."

Although I didn't see the benefits back then, not a day goes by that I'm not grateful for my parents' decision to have me and my siblings in America, raise us back in Nigeria, and allow us the freedom to come back to the States if we wanted to. When I returned at seventeen for college, despite some of the stereotypical biases I endured, I understood the privilege I also had. That didn't mean I didn't work hard to get to where I was. But I was aware and tried not to take my opportunities for granted.

"Okay, cool—"

"A formal congrats, Nyce, on being named global ambassador for the Basketball Africa League."

I clasped my hands together and nodded with a smile on my face. This was the good news I got right before I walked into the meeting. I'd been doing some work with the Nigerian team for years. And it was such a huge honor to represent BAL, which was a partnership between the NBA and FIBU in Africa. The league had its inaugural season some years ago. For my efforts to be noticed, and then being tapped to help expand Africa's footprint around the world was a huge deal.

"Thanks, man. What you about to get into?" I asked.

"I got a few more meetings to attend, so I think I'mma hang out in my suite for the night."

"You know you too young to be this boring?" I laughed at my own joke while Marcus waved me off. I wasn't sure exactly how old he was, but I knew he was in his mid-forties.

"Maybe if you started acting how old you are, Amara and I wouldn't have these gray hairs," he snapped.

Shrugging, I inclined my head toward him. "Y'all have gray

hairs cause you respond to everything that doesn't need y'all's energy."

"I'm not going there with you. If you do go out tonight, please take Terry and don't get into any trouble. We're almost at the finish line."

Terry was the bodyguard I traveled with most of the time. Marcus knew that sometimes, I also liked to roll solo on my incognito tip. "Man, my dad is in Enugu. Besides, I'm always chilling in the cut. These groupies be looking for me."

Marcus shook his head as we walked out of the conference room heading towards the elevators that led to the lobby. Two opposing opinions could be right at the same time, and I wasn't backing down from mine. My boy, Niyi DaSilva, was in town doing a listening party for his new solo project. He was part of the award-winning Christian Neo Soul group, 891 Project that had recently retired after completing their last world tour. He now had a Christian R&B EP that would drop soon. He hit me up that he was in town, so I was about to fall through. At first, I wasn't sure I'd be in NYC, but since I was here, I was going to support my guy.

"You gotta go to Rwanda for this BAL thing—"

"Okay, send me the dates and I'll let Ci know so she can work it to coincide with when I'm in Nigeria."

Marcus cut his eyes at me, and I knew why. I laughed and waved him off. Ciara was Arinze's assistant, but I preferred her doing stuff for me rather than the assistant assigned to me by the agency. Ci, as we called her, was part of the family. Although she stayed extorting me any chance she got, she was good people. I was going to have to give her and her punk boyfriend some courtside tickets for the new season.

A few hours later, I was back in my suite at the Ritz. I had an early dinner and now needed a shower so I could head back out. The listening party was in one upscale club in Brooklyn. I decided to heed Marcus's advice, so I hit Terry up to let him know that we needed to roll out at seven. Based on the time, I had roughly two hours to get ready.

Discarding my clothes, I headed to the bathroom. Setting my phone on the charger, I started the shower. I was looking forward to a long, hot one because it was my time to think. Stepping in, I closed my eyes and let out a sigh as the hot water massaged my muscles. I didn't have enough time to soak after my work out this morning, so I was still sore.

"Y'all, lissen, after all I went through at the airport. My luggage and…ugh. I don't even wanna think about it. The bottom line is, your girl got here, and they upgraded my room. Here, let me show y'all."

I'd turned off the shower when I heard a voice. It sounded familiar, but it couldn't be. I tied a towel around my waist and picked up another to hang around my neck. With my feet in my slippers, I crept to the door.

"Family…can't nobody tell me that God is not good. He was looking out for me. I have this big thing I hope to share with y'all later but…oh man, check out this view."

I opened the door and peeped out. Clear as day, there stood Reign Davis. She was telling somebody about her room. Except it wasn't hers. I sauntered out, creeping up behind her. She didn't respond to my text earlier, so this was a welcome surprise. Unexpected, but definitely welcome. I lowered my face and whispered in her ear.

"Hey baby, I see you did me one better."

Reign yelled and turned around. I peeped at her phone. She wasn't on a call. She was LIVE on IG. She struggled to regain her composure so she could end the session, but her camera was now on me. Snapping into action, I took the phone from her and turned it off.

"Oh my gosh. Cheta, what are you doing in my room? And please put on a shirt!"

"As much as I want it to be, this ain't your room, Reign."

I watched as the fear in her brown eyes morphed into confusion before finally settling on annoyance. Someone had some explaining to do, but I couldn't front like I wasn't happy to see her.

4

———

REIGN

I was sure my heart was about to explode out of my chest. One, because this man just scared the living daylights out of me, and two, he looked like a three-course meal put together by a world-class chef. His voice and the fact that his broad chest still had droplets of water from his shower weren't helping matters. Neither was the white towel tied loosely around his waist. I was in a fight for my life, willing my eyes not to venture to his lower extremities. I placed my hand over my eyes since I couldn't trust them to do right.

"Put on a shirt!"

When I didn't hear movement, I peeked to see what he was doing. Cheta's big arms were folded across his chest while he looked down at me. In his eyes was a challenge.

"I'mma need you to ask again." With his index finger and thumb slightly apart, he leaned in. "But with less bass in your voice."

I knew this wasn't the time to dare him. So, I tried another approach. "Please…" I pleaded, softly.

"Better."

I looked at the keycard in my hand. It did say the Royal Suite. I felt Cheta still hovering over me. "What?"

"I didn't think voyeurism was your thing, but if it is..." His hand went to his towel.

Wait, what? My brows furrowed. This man had me so flustered that I was losing my mind. Then I realized I was in the bedroom. I scurried away, his laughter trailing behind me. *Jerk.*

"I'll be ready in a minute, then we can go downstairs and see what's up."

I walked into the living room and sat on the beige sofa. My mind raced as to how this could happen. I knew that the virtual temp assistant Ebonie hired made a few mistakes when she first started, but I double checked the reservation myself. There were a little over a hundred people on my LIVE when Cheta ended it abruptly. I ran through possible explanations in case someone did recognize him. It was unlikely, but you never knew.

The reason I was here on Friday, even though my meeting was Monday, was that I didn't want to be flustered. I wanted to use the weekend to take in some of New York and be well rested. Over the past few weeks, I'd worked day and night perfecting everything.

"Let's go."

I lifted my eyes to him, and his pupils flared with desire. He sauntered toward me, causing my breath to hitch. Yeah, there was a reason I stayed far away from him. He knew he looked good and was aware of his effect on women. Standing, I exited out of my fog. I reminded myself that like a decadent chocolate brownie, I couldn't hang around him too long without being tempted. Temptation always came with possible side effects.

Of their own accord, my eyes roamed his frame. At first glance, the light army green sweater he wore over black pants looked casual. But I was sure they were designer's labels. The black rubber soled sneakers were the reason I didn't hear him approach. His platinum watch and single Cuban link were the only pieces of jewelry he had on. I wanted to roll my luggage out, but he told me to leave them until we got everything sorted out. Cheta ushered me out of the room, and we headed to the elevators.

It didn't take us long to get things straightened out at the front desk. I was now freshly showered and in my rightful room. The day had been pure trash. I wanted to throw it all away. The current plan was to eat and forget about the day. While I waited for room service, I called my sister.

Wrapping my locs up in a messy bun, I rolled my eyes again at the now irritating sound of her laughter. Ebonie would've been more sympathetic toward my situation, but she was in London, and I needed to vent. Deja thought it was funny, but nothing about what I'd endured since I boarded my plane to NYC earlier was.

My sister was with me in the shop last week when the lunch Cheta ordered arrived. I successfully dodged her questions, but when his flowers arrived last weekend, I couldn't avoid them anymore. So, I ended up narrating the Cheta story from the beginning. She agreed with Ebonie that I should give him a chance. But that wasn't happening.

"I'm on the website now. The room you booked was 425 square feet. How did you think they'd upgrade you to a 2,175 square-foot suite?" Deja asked.

It did sound incredulous, but that's exactly what I thought. After I'd had to wait at the airport because my luggage was delayed, then sit through horrible traffic to get here, I believed that God was rewarding me. For all those times I held my tongue and didn't cuss people out today.

"I'm about to hang up on you with all this laughing. I thought it was my well done from God—"

"You see, you starting to sound like our mother. Y'all think God does everything. He does the impossible, but not that."

I walked back into the living area of the new suite the hotel gave me. Ever since college, I traveled any chance I got. My preferred low budget hotel was owned by Marriott, which also owned the Ritz. I knew that I'd ask for an upgrade once I got here with all the points I had accumulated. So, when they gave me the Royal Suite, I didn't too much question it.

When we got to the lobby earlier, the clerk was stammering and couldn't explain what happened. I watched as Cheta's patience began to slip and he tried to hem the clerk up. I hurriedly asked him to call the manager. When she appeared, the woman recognized Cheta at once. She also had no shame in openly lusting over him as she escorted us to her office. There she explained what happened.

It was just my luck that they'd experienced a system glitch several minutes before I arrived. The clerk was a relatively new hire so when he upgraded me, he mistakenly upgraded me to a bigger room than what my points allowed for. The glitch had Cheta's room showing as vacant and clean. So that's where I ended up. The suite was gorgeous, and I was so in awe that I didn't even hear the shower. Then I thought the smart thing to do was go LIVE. I wanted to testify since I had been complaining on Twitter all day.

"Well, what's done is done. How was the shop today?" I asked since she was manning the shop for me until I returned on Wednesday.

"The shop is fine, but we aren't changing the topic. So where is Mr. NBA now?"

I shrugged. "How am I supposed to know? Once they gave me my real suite, I got my luggage out of his room and let him go about his business."

"You know you don't lie very well."

She was right. I did know where he was. He was at a listening party in Brooklyn which he'd invited me to, and I promptly declined. The paparazzi followed that man like he was the only celeb in America. Although he promised to keep me hidden, I couldn't risk being seen with him.

I knew people changed. Jasmine vouched countless times that her fiancé said his cousin had done a 180. A complete about-face from his philandering and reckless ways. Still, I couldn't risk the affiliation. Not now, and most likely never. He was a sweet man though. I watched as his tone shifted from hard and brash when he addressed other people to soft and accommodating when he talked to me. It was also not lost on me that he wasn't as angry that someone had walked into his room as he was that I might've entered the room of someone who could harm me because of their mistake.

"Be that as it may. I'm here for business and I'm focused only on that. Besides, he's leaving for Atlanta in the morning."

Deja sighed. I knew she wanted to say more on the topic, but I was glad she didn't. We talked a little bit more about every and anything. I was truly enjoying having my sister stateside. After a few more minutes, there was a knock on my door. My stomach growled at the thought of my spiced lamb kebab with tabbouleh. I stayed on the phone with my sister as the food was wheeled in. I tipped the server and he left.

"Dee, I gotta go. I'm starving."

"Okay, sis. I love you and I'm proud of you. Remember I have a wedding to attend in the evening. So, I'll leave the shop before closing, but Lula said she'll be okay."

I removed the cloche and the aroma wafted up my nostrils. "Have fun! She'll be fine and knows to call me if she needs me. I appreciate you and I love you too." I disconnected the call and sat to say grace as my phone buzzed again.

Cheta: Checking in. You good?

I couldn't help the way my lips turned up in a smile. I could no longer leave him on read even if I wanted to.

Yes, thanks for asking. Hope you're having fun.

Cheta: Woulda been better if you'd joined me. But it's cool.

Heat prickled my skin. Against my blaring common sense screaming no, I decided to goad him.

We can't all have what we want.

Cheta: LOL...I can, and I intend to

I swallowed against the tightness in my throat. Lifting my hand, I rubbed the back of my neck. Deciding that was enough of living on the wild side for one night, I responded:

Goodnight Cheta. Have a safe flight back

He sent a couple of laughing emojis accompanied by:

You stay looking for the exit. I'mma let you make it. Sweet dreams, Rei baby.

I set the phone down, relieved that he "let me make it." I started my relaxation playlist and began to enjoy my meal. As much as I tried to evict him, Cheta occupied all parts of my mind.

For the umpteenth time, I pinched myself. I was seated in Coleman Hospitality Group's office on Sixth Avenue in NYC. There was another person that was pitching with me. We'd been served coffee and pastries. After that, we were given a tour of the office building. Then we got settled into this conference room where the VP of Acquisitions came in and talked about the history of Coleman and its locations. This was information I already knew because I studied this company like I had a final exam coming. I couldn't contain my excitement and anxiety.

Unlike my arrival in NYC, the weekend was perfect. On Saturday morning, I was surprised with breakfast delivered to my room. Cheta sent it. There was a little of everything. After eating, I got dressed and headed out to take in the sights and sounds of the city. The following day, I listened to online service as I walked around Central Park. When I got back to the hotel, I looked over my presentation and then relaxed. I had done all I could, so now I was in surrender mode.

I watched in awe as *the* Monica Coleman-Hunt talked about the vision of Coleman Hospitality and her commitment to Black brands. She emphasized her position on not compromising the value and reputation of her company to help the brands because they were black, but giving them the space and opportunity they otherwise wouldn't have to showcase their excellence.

The yellow business suit she had on complimented her rich, dark chocolate skin. Her gorgeous afro was in a mohawk style. Her average height was enhanced by black stilettos. Four men walked behind her as she entered the room earlier. Three of them I now knew worked for her. The other I wasn't so sure. I didn't think I'd get to see her, but I was thankful I did. Her command of the room was inspiring.

We were told that because of infringement concerns, the presentations would be done separately. Also, because they wanted to show good faith, we were presented with a mutual, non-disclosure agreement. Once Monica concluded her speech, I was told to step outside while the other business stayed to give their presentation. A part of me wanted to feel intimidated when the men entered the room earlier. Ebonie couldn't be here, so I was by my lonesome. But that didn't mean I didn't intend to kill it.

Kill it is exactly what I did. A few hours later, I stood in front of the bank of elevators with the VP of Acquisitions. I'd done my presentation and I felt so good about it. Well, that was after I shifted from one leg to the other while wringing my fingers until they hurt. When Monica cleared her throat, I swung into action.

"Beautiful skin requires a commitment, not a miracle," I'd started.

That was my opening and apparently the icebreaker I needed. After light laughter, I moved on to explaining all the products included in the Lush by BGE package. I set up the model display. The new packaging came out great. I detailed each product, the ingredients, and their benefits. I took questions before I talked about Coleman's existing customer demographics and the benefits we'd provide.

I had a rush of energy when Monica's lips lifted in a small smile. While I concluded with time frame expectations upon receipt of a potential contract, I passed around my samples. Monica had to leave before I was done, and I almost let that knock me off my square. Considering I didn't even think she would be there, I shook off my worries and closed it out.

The elevators opened and I turned to shake the VP's hand before stepping in. "Thank you again for the opportunity."

"You're welcome and I'm glad I had the opportunity to meet you," he said.

I hit the button to go to the lobby. Adjusting the strap of my portfolio, I smiled as I waited for the door to close.

"For what it's worth, Monica was impressed."

I wanted to ask more, but the door closed. I was sure he wasn't supposed to tell me that, but I was so glad he did. Pulling out my phone, I ordered an Uber and then called Ebonie, but my call went straight to voicemail. She was on her way back to the US, so must still be in the air.

My flight was for six a.m., and now I was wondering what I had to have been smoking to set it that early. I exited the building to the warmth from the sun's rays soothing my skin. I took in a long breath and exhaled. I had no idea why offices kept their buildings so cold. A few minutes later, the Uber pulled up. I got in and rested my head against the headrest, trying to calm my nerves from the events of the past seventy-two hours.

I flipped my phone in my hand, and the gnawing feeling I'd had since I woke up this morning returned. I hadn't heard from Cheta since I thanked him for breakfast on Saturday. I knew I shouldn't, but I felt some type of way. He'd been all over me, well as much as someone who I was ignoring could be. And now that I was less resistant, he suddenly went silent. After he badgered me, I had shared with him a little bit of what I was doing here. He seemed genuinely interested, but I guess that was all an act. I could text him, but I nixed the idea immediately.

Several minutes later, I was back in my room. I flung my shoes off my feet and wiggled my toes. Slipping into my slippers, I placed my food on the table and turned on the TV. Logging into my Netflix account, I found my show, *L.A's Finest*, and went to wash my hands. The hotel phone rang, and it was from the front desk telling me I had a delivery. Minutes later, there was a knock on my door and the most beautiful bouquet of roses and hydrangeas was handed to me. The note read:

I trust you kicked their collective corporate behind. No slackers on my team

My cheeks began to hurt, a sign I was smiling too hard. He remembered. I wanted to call him, but I decided to do it when I was well rested.

The following day, I stepped into Hartsfield Jackson airport and hurried to catch the train to baggage claim. I had to do better at this traveling thing. My being well rested turned into the television watching me as I fell asleep right after dinner. In the weeks preparing for NYC, granted I barely got six hours of sleep daily, but I shouldn't be that tired.

I woke up a little after four a.m., hurriedly packed, took a shower, and ordered an Uber right before my phone died. I barely made it to the airport to check in and charge my phone for a few minutes when I had to board.

As I was resting next to the train door, my phone started to buzz. It was Ebonie. I answered, but the service was shaky so it wouldn't connect. Once the train stopped, I got off, made my way to the escalator and started to dial Ebonie when her text came through instead.

CALL ME NOW!

As I swiped to call her, my phone started buzzing like crazy.

The service was now better, so all the notifications were coming through. I was getting tagged on Twitter and Instagram. I stood to the side and opened Instagram. My heart thudded as I read the first caption I was tagged in.

"Seems Like Nyce Is Back To Playing Not So Nice."

There was a screenshot of a shirtless Cheta behind me in his hotel room. He had his hands on my waist and a grin plastered on his face. Worst of all, he was looking at me like he wanted to devour me. This was not good. I wanted the ground to open and swallow me. They knew who I was because it was my Instagram account. I stumbled back against the wall. The airport seemed to spin as I struggled to steady my breathing.

My phone rang. Ebonie was calling back.

"Eb, this can't be happening." My voice shook as I willed back tears.

"Rei, where are you?"

"I'm—"

"Ms. Davis?"

"Eb, hold on…" I frowned at the freakishly tall, bulky man staring down at me. "Who wants to know?"

"My name is Izaak, Mr. Kalu sent me."

I furrowed my brows. I put my phone back to my ear as anger seared through me. "Eb, I'm at the airport, but I got this guy that says Cheta sent him. I'm going to kill that man, I swear."

"Rei, I know you're shaken up, but openly admitting to wanting to commit murder isn't a good look. Keep me on the phone and see what he wants."

I looked up at him. "What?" He didn't do anything to me, but everyone associated with Cheta could get this work.

His stance was like that of someone in the military. Both hands in front of him, legs apart. "I was instructed to take you to where you want to go."

Before he left New York, Cheta and I chatted briefly about my return. So, he knew when I'd be landing and that I had

Uber'ed. But I wanted no parts of him. Not now. "No, thank you."

Izaak took out his phone and dialed. Seconds later, he handed me the phone. My gaze floated past him. I took in a breath, lifted my brow, and refocused. His expression remained aplomb at my hesitation. Rolling my eyes, I took the phone.

"Reign?"

"What, Cheta?" I shouted.

"Bring it down a few, baby. I'm out of town, but I need you to go with Iz," he said, calmly.

"No, thank you. Do you see what they're saying? I just want to go home and continue with my normal life."

"I know you do, but now, you can't. I'll be back tomorrow night. Until then, let him take you to my house."

I furrowed my brows. "Wait. What? No. I'm going home, and then my shop." I heard Ebonie say something, so I put my phone to my ear. "What?"

"The paparazzi are stationed outside the shop. I got a call from the landlord when he couldn't reach you," she said.

I let out a large sigh. I turned back to Izaak. "Cheta, I'm so angry with you."

"I know. We can discuss whose fault it is and what to do when I see you. If you don't go to my house, let him take you to yours. He'll be on you until I get back."

I remained silent.

"Reign?"

"I hear you. Can I go now?"

He sniggered.

There was nothing at all funny about this. My thoughts moved to my family. If my parents got wind of this, which they eventually would, a sermon about fornication was in my near future.

"I gotta go. Don't give that man a hard time. His job is to do everything to keep you safe. Everything. Don't try me, please."

I hung up on him and handed the phone to the Izaak guy. "Eb, let me get my bags. I'll be home in an hour."

"I'll meet you there."

I rolled my eyes as I felt Izaak's presence behind me. I needed Cheta's team to put out some kind of statement so I could go on about my business.

5

CHETA

*R*eign cut her eyes at me before returning her hard glare to my publicist, Amara. It'd been two days since Reign and I hit the blogs and the frenzy hadn't died down yet. Every couple of hours, *The Shade Space* and *Tatafo Tales* posted the picture with a different caption. Other blogs followed suit, with the usual copy and paste. No one had a different angle.

I was used to it. Reign wasn't. She hadn't said two words to me since I talked to her at the airport. I didn't know what she was so mad at me for. She walked into *my* room. How was I supposed to know she was on IG LIVE? I get she needed someone to blame, and I'd be that. But I was sick of her side eyes.

As mad as she was, she still looked beautiful. Today she had on a sleeveless, white dress and her locs were swooped to the side. She was here with a lady she introduced as her business partner, Ebonie Smith.

We were in the LST offices in downtown Atlanta. I steepled my fingers under my lip and leaned back in my chair. Marcus sat by my side, while Reign and her friend were on the opposite side of the table. Amara was stationed at the head with her hand on her hip. She pulled no punches with me before they arrived about

49

an hour ago. She talked about how my recklessness had put the ESPN deal, my ambassadorship, and the upcoming season all on the line.

Amara was like a cool big sister who wasn't afraid to kick my behind. She was one of the best publicists out there. But there was only so much scolding I was going to take from someone who wasn't my mama. In hindsight, I wasn't thinking. But again, I didn't expect Reign to be live on Instagram. That's the issue with social media. Everyone had to show the world what they were doing at all times of the day.

"Look, I don't know why you can't release a statement to clear this whole thing up," Reign said. "We've been here for an hour, and I've told you what happened."

Amara looked at me then cut her eyes to Reign. "Oh, I'm sorry. I didn't know you were also a publicist." She dramatically put her hand on her chest. "I must have missed that."

"No need to be cute—" Reign started.

"Then don't tell me how to do my job," Amara snapped.

"Okay. Reign, chill," Ebonie said. "If a statement won't do, then what?"

Amara stood up straight. She looked at me and I already knew nonsense was about to come out of her mouth.

"This is bigger than a simple statement. My client can't afford to be tied to another woman with no real commitment. A casual date is one thing. Half-naked in a hotel room is another. After the most recent debacle…" She shook her head. "No, not now. The hotel will never admit to the world that they made a mistake and let some woman into their guest's room. One who happens to be the current MVP of the NBA. Even if they did, no one would believe that story."

My eyes darted to Reign. Her face contoured and her teeth clenched. I was sure she thought Amara didn't believe her story either. I narrowed my eyes at Amara who had told me to remain quiet during the meeting. She waved me off and continued.

"The latest picture of you two, which was posted two hours ago, came with a snippet of audio. How that happened, I have no idea, but Mr. Kalu can be heard saying something. How do I spin it? How will the world believe that you're not some groupie who's after him? Especially since they've never seen you before."

Reign sat up straight. "What?"

Amara put her hands on her hip. "Let me spell it out for you. Cheta has worked really hard the past few years to clean up his reputation. I've worked hard to clean up his reputation."

She rolled her eyes and turned to me. "We were doing great until that incident with the fake baby mamas last year. We're just getting past that and now this. We can't take a step backward. There's too much on the line right now. You need to be set for your post NBA days."

I rubbed my forehead, knowing she was talking about the ESPN deal.

"There've been too many women, too many pregnancy scares, too many thirsty women thinking they were about to become the next NBA wife, then got disappointed and wanted to get revenge... Too many rumors." She threw her hands in the air and I really understood the stress I had caused her over the years.

She repeated herself. "Again, we can't have yet another woman and no commitment. You're thirty-five, headed into retirement. You won't be able to gain respect with your game anymore. When people aren't ignoring your crazy personal life because you're magic on the court, what do you think will happen to you?"

She let out a deep breath. "I'm trying to set you up for the long haul here, Cheta. And you're doing everything you can to thwart that."

I hung my head. "This wasn't my fault. Not saying it was hers. It was a crazy coincidence."

Amara pressed her lips together, looking a little less irritated. "I get that. And I'm sorry. But it still has to be fixed." She took a deep breath and a long pause. I knew that whatever she was about to say, I wasn't gonna like.

She finally shrugged and said, "The only option for both of you is a fake engagement."

"What?"

"*Mba!!*"

"Are you kidding me?"

I shook my head as Ebonie, I, and Reign responded simultaneously. Marcus was eerily quiet, meaning he knew about this.

I was attracted to Reign. I wouldn't wish her harm, but I wasn't sure if I even liked her as a person. Primarily because I didn't know her. There was no way I was going to agree to be engaged to her. I knew it would be fake, but that still needed work I wasn't ready to put in.

"Look it'll be only for a year. It's not as lasting as a marriage, and neither is it as casual as a girlfriend. The story will be that you've been seeing each other, but wanted to keep it very quiet," Amara continued.

Reign packed up her bag. "No. I'm not doing it."

Ebonie looked down at her phone and shook her head. I wondered what that was about. She looked at Reign. "Reign, you need to sit."

"No, and I cannot believe you want me to stay and listen to this. And you…" she turned to me. "All of a sudden, you're mute?! Was this your plan all along?"

Anger traveled up my spine. I furrowed my brows. "Don't flatter yourself, woman."

How dare she? She was mad, but what wasn't about to happen was her trying to act like I orchestrated the whole thing. She was fine, but not that fine. I could have any woman I wanted, and I didn't need to force someone to get engaged to me. I reeled in my temper, so I didn't hurt her feelings. She tried it though and it was in her best interest to look for something safe to do.

Ebonie tugged her arm and whispered something in her ear.

Reign's eyes bugged, then sadness washed over them. I was about to speak when Ebonie spoke.

"Can you give us a few minutes?"

Not waiting for an answer, she took Reign by the arm, and they left the room.

Amara turned to me. "Cheta, you need to get on board. Let me paint a clearer picture for you." She pulled out her iPad, and after a few taps and swipes, she got to what she was looking for.

Leaning over the table, she said, "Look at this…"

I moved forward and she began swiping her device. There were up to ten or so sleazy blogs that had a different caption for the same photo. One went so far as to talk about the women in my hotel room a couple of years ago, saying I was at it again and wondering how long it would be before we were waiting for a DNA test for Reign's baby. Another painted a horrible picture of me trying to ruin a wholesome Christian girl. The issue now was that reputable media outlets were picking up the story. I don't know what it was about my wet chest they found so fascinating. I hissed and pushed away from the table.

"You say you don't care, but deep down you do. Forget the fame, before anything else, you're Igbo. We value the family name and you…" she pointed at me, "…have allowed yours to be stained for far too long.

"Now, let's talk about fame, success, and your future. For years, your fan base let you get away with a lot. Your rise in stardom has changed that. You're now one of, if not the, most recognizable Nigerian basketballers in the NBA. That comes with being open to public judgment. Those voices are very loud and will cancel you without a second thought. You know this and that's why you hired me to manage the perception of your image. You need to do this, so we can get her on board," she said with finality.

An argument laced my tongue, but I bit it back. Amara was also Igbo and was spot on with the culture thing and the other points. I'd never heard of her until Marcus brought her on, but she'd been a lifesaver. Maturity and age demanded I got myself together. I didn't want to be another has-been athlete that faded to obscurity once my active career was over. There would always be opportunities, but not premium ones.

"Nicholas over at ESPN already told me there've been whispers since this story broke. We need to fix this now," Marcus added.

The door opened and Reign and Ebonie reentered. Reign didn't meet my eyes. As much as it pained me to follow Amara's directive of not speaking, I remained silent.

"What's it going to be?" Amara asked, once they took their seats.

"Why does the arrangement have to be so long?" Ebonie asked.

"In two and a half months, the NBA season will start. I won't have my client with a broken engagement before the season ends for him. Be it April for regular season or June for the finals."

"Amara, you don't have faith in me. That's cold." I didn't know what she thought, but the championship was coming home.

She narrowed her eyes at me. "Not now."

"And you're certain there's no other way? Because I don't see what Reign is getting out of this." Ebonie folded her arms across her chest. It seemed like she was now the spokesperson because Reign remained silent.

Amara stared at Ebonie for a few seconds. "We don't have time for this."

She then turned to Reign, who lifted her eyes. "Nothing personal, Ms. Davis, but I protect my client above anything else. I did my research; I know why you were in NYC. You have two options, be his makeshift fiancée for twelve months, or I'll pull out all stops to paint you as a groupie looking for her next come up. I wonder what Monica Coleman-Hunt's thoughts will be of the person they're thinking of going into business with."

Amara returned her eyes to Ebonie. "Me playing nice, that's what she gets out of this."

Reign gasped and tears danced in her eyes.

My heart constricted. She'd pissed me off, but her tears were where I drew the line. "Amara…"

She turned to me. "This can't be another 'he's misunderstood' story. I signed on to protect you, even if it's from you."

I got it. I really did. She'd been repeating it for the past two hours, but I couldn't salvage my image at Reign's expense. I needed to talk to her. "Reign and I need the room."

Reign raised her head. Her tired eyes closed in defeat. She'd had a lot of fight until Ebonie whispered something to her earlier.

"Cheta…"

"Amara, *anụla m gị*. I got this. I need the room."

Minutes later, everyone shuffled out and the weight in the room was suffocating. Reign lowered her head.

"Aye, come here."

She lifted her head and stared at me, but didn't move.

"Please come here."

She let out an exaggerated breath, then stood and walked over. I pulled out the chair Marcus left vacant and told her to sit. She did and I pulled the chair in between my long legs so she was encased in.

"Talk to me."

"About what? If I don't agree, your publicist will spread lies about me." She rolled her eyes. "I can't stand her. I want to cuss her out so bad."

I chuckled. "Amara's doing her job. It's not personal. She let me have it before you got here. And I pay her!"

My joke brought a tiny smile to her face. She sighed again. "Coleman Hospitality is a faith and family type of business. They've already seen the picture. I may be disqualified. I'm so tired of getting knocked down." She covered her face with her hands and bent her head.

I lifted her head with my index finger. "Hey, didn't I tell you there're no slackers on my team? Is that what Ebonie was telling you?"

"Yes, as we were talking, she got an email inquiring about the incident. They wanted to hear from me first."

"So, rather than a fake engagement, you're willing to give up all your hard work? I must be ugly then, or do I smell? Maybe it's my teeth…they crooked, aren't they?"

Reign laughed and hit me on my forearm. "Stop. This isn't funny."

"It's not, but it is what it is. It's not like you'll be living with me…or wait, you want to?"

She frowned. "Absolutely not."

"But you gotta kiss me though. I'm going to enjoy that." I winked.

She didn't protest and I banked that in my mental. There was no denying our attraction. But I also knew being with me was going to be a major shift for her. One I wasn't sure she fully understood at this time.

"Why didn't I just go to my regular hotel?" she asked.

"I can't answer that, but you know the generic cliché my cousins always spit out when things don't go my way?"

Her brows knit together. "No?"

"Everything happens for a reason. So, there's your answer. Look at it this way, I can help you with Coleman—"

"No, I don't want—"

"Whoa…chill. I meant *when* you get it, not *if*, my celebrity can help. But you did that Reign, not anybody else. You. So, stand on that and be proud. This can be mutually beneficial."

There was a tap on the door. It was Amara. She probably thought I had sold my soul. I waved her in. Everyone else entered and took a seat. Reign remained by my side.

"What's it going to be?" Amara asked.

Silence filled the room as everyone looked at Reign.

"I'll do it."

"Good." Amara put her hand in her bag, produced a tiny velvet box and slid it to me. My eyes bugged as I looked at what had to be about two or three carats. The cut though I knew was round. I knew this because I went with Arinze to buy Jasmine's ring. My real wife would get nothing less than five carats, but this would do.

"You knew I was going to agree, huh?" Reign sassed.

"Like I said, I've been doing this for almost twenty years." Amara turned to me. "I'll send you the bill for that."

"Nah, that's on you. You coulda gone to Walmart for a cubic zirconia. This looks like it's custom. She's not even marrying me for real."

Reign gasped and I waggled my brows at her.

"Anyway…" Amara continued. "Let's get down to the details. First, the only people that'll know of this arrangement are the people in this room."

We all nodded in agreement, then she continued. "You two seem to have some kind of relationship, so I'll leave the specifics of your dates to you. The following, though, is a must. You must be seen together at least four to five times a month. Remember you're engaged—act like it. You both live in the city, so that makes it easier. Two weeks in advance, I'll send over any events that you absolutely must attend together. Once the season starts, Ms. Davis, you'll have to attend all home games and at least one away game a month. All expenses will be covered. Travel…you guys need to go on vacation together. For the immediate future, Cheta's going to Nigeria in a few weeks and Ms. Davis, you'll have to accompany him."

"Huh? Why?" she asked.

"His dad is being conferred with a chieftaincy title. He's the only son. Once the news hits, it'll scream fake if his fiancée is absent from such a huge family celebration."

Reign stared at me. Her eyes were laced with fear as she sported a deep frown.

"We'll talk." I checked my watch. I was picking my niece up since her dad was out of town. Her nanny could do it, but I promised her. I hated to leave with things still crazy, but I couldn't leave Uju hanging.

"You must follow each other on social media. Post each other at least once a week. You must leave comments under each other's post as well. Whether it's a post about each other or other things in your life. Cheta, if she posts business, repost at least once a month. I'm sure I'll get requests for an interview. I'll thoroughly vet—"

I grunted and shook my head. "Amara, you know I don't do media. Because of the circumstance, I'll speak to one outlet. One." Just because I got fake engaged didn't mean I liked those jokers to be talking to them like we were friends. Nah, my stance was non-negotiable.

"We'll talk—"

"You're not hearing me. I'm not bending, I'll only sit with one outlet."

Seeing she wasn't going to win this one, Amara turned to Ebonie. "Ms. Smith, I'll need you to be sort of a buffer for Ms. Davis."

"A what?"

"Being her business partner and friend, and the only one that should know about this, I'll need you to post pictures about them occasionally and comment under their posts."

Ebonie shook her head. "Wow…y'all think of everything…huh?"

Amara shrugged. "Ms. Davis, an expense account will be opened, and the card FedExed to you. Everything pertaining to your role for its duration should come out of this account."

Amara reiterated that we were both supposed to fully play our parts. Reign almost fainted when she thought that included sex. Amara clarified it didn't but added that I couldn't indulge with anyone else and risk getting caught by paparazzi either. I wasn't about to go without sex for a year, but I was going to let her believe she had the upper hand for now.

"I have something to add." Reign pinned me with her gaze. "I know you're rich and famous. I'm way outta my league, here. But I'm trusting you with my image. Please, don't embarrass me or my family. Don't have me out here looking like a clown. I don't have a team that will help me clean it up."

My chest tightened. It was almost as though she was appealing to a deeper side of me. I took in a breath and leaned forward. I needed her to hear me say this. "Understood and I gotchu."

She nodded.

For the next several minutes, a contract, NDAs, and some other papers were signed. Amara read a statement that she would release. After Reign and I made some adjustments, we agreed to its contents. Reign had given me her trust and I knew how hard of a commodity that was to come by. My initial plan was to keep doing me, but now I had another person to consider. This was the reason I wasn't in a real relationship. At this moment, I realized this was about to be a headache I wasn't sure I was ready to deal with.

6

REIGN

The timer on the microwave went off. I opened it and retrieved the bag of popcorn inside. Drawing the bowl closer, I held the bag by the tip, shook, and opened it. The steam from the buttered popcorn filled my kitchen. It was Friday evening and Deja and I were having a movie night. Going out wasn't an option and since she'd be headed back to Spain next weekend, movie night it was. Initially, Cheta wanted to make plans for us, but I declined. I understood it was something I had to do, but this was more important. To make it up to him, I'd be spending the day with him tomorrow.

The Amara lady gave us a day...a measly day before she released the statement. I really did want to curse her out. It was her job, but she didn't have to be so rude about it. After I signed the next year of my life away, Cheta had to run to get his niece. He wanted me to come with him, but I needed to decompress from the hamster wheel I'd been on. I did request an NDA for my sister to sign. There was no way I could keep this from her. Cheta agreed with me. I guess because his cousins were going to know about it as well.

That evening, when Ebonie and I arrived at my house, I

updated Deja. After she got over the initial shock and horror, she couldn't stop laughing at me. "That man has wanted you for months. You must've pissed Cupid off because babeee... I ain't never heard of this kind of coincidence in my life," Deja had said.

Ebonie who was just as mad as me when the whole thing was unfolding in that conference room, now thought it was funny too. My brother was stunned, but happy for me. My parents, on the other hand, had me on the phone for an hour about my knack for being reckless. One mistake when I was a teenager and they never let me forget it. I let them have their say because there was no way I'd tell them the truth. They, like the rest of the world, would remain clueless.

I'd taken the day after all that drama off, but after that, I had a business to run. I fought tooth and nail for my life to remain as normal as possible. When I got to the shop the following morning, I was in for a rude awakening. I thought I could brave it, but I had a hard time getting into my shop with folks trying to stop me. I knew most of them wanted to see the person that *got* their hometown hero to settle down. But it was so strange that people wanted to know about someone else's life that bad.

Later, when Cheta asked about my day, I mistakenly let out my frustration about the paparazzi outside my shop. After he told me I was hardheaded, Izaak appeared at my doorstep the following morning. I've had a driver slash personal security ever since.

One week had gone by and I still couldn't recognize my life. I stared at the ring on my finger. It was a three-carat, round cut diamond. Simply gorgeous. But even after a week of wearing it, my hand still felt like it belonged to someone else. I rolled my eyes when I remembered Cheta refusing to put it on my finger. Instead, he kissed my forehead and said, "The only finger I'm putting a ring on belongs to the woman who's gonna be my wife and the mother of my kids...for real."

I didn't know how to take him sometimes. He acted like he

had no sense, but he did. He graduated with top honors in Mechanical Engineering. Knew when to behave, but opted not to sometimes. He had a temper that simmered at the surface but once it was out, oh boy. I saw that when some random commented on about twenty of my posts. The person had a lot of time because they went down my grid and decided to be vile.

Cheta blew a gasket when Amara told him he couldn't respond. He hated responding to the press or comments he called stupid, but was willing to respond in my defense. It was sweet, but I dared not call him sweet. How I went from minding my own business to the whole world trying to mind mine, I couldn't even fathom. Not only was I in almost every American blog, but I was also in African blogs. Specifically, Nigeria.

Everyone had an opinion about me, about Cheta, and our "engagement." Some kinda liked me, some couldn't stand the ground I walked on. I tried not to take it to heart because as Cheta liked to say, the only opinion that mattered was his. But he could afford to say that. He was famous and like it or not, a man.

Why couldn't he be like his cousins? Arinze was a well-established actor, but he was low key. Jidenna, to me, was scary. There was always more to the quiet types. I'd met them when Jasmine opened her flower shop last year. I hadn't seen them recently, but Cheta had Facetimed them when I saw him the day before. Of course, they teased me. Everyone knew how Cheta chased and I ran.

"Are we watching this or you're going to keep staring into space?" Deja leaned on the door frame.

I snickered and grabbed the bowl from the counter. "Grab the wine. I thought you were still on the phone with Juan."

She went to the refrigerator, and I got some paper towels. "How serious is this thing between the two of you anyway? I get he makes you happy, but—"

She shrugged. "I like him, a lot. I'm having fun, but you know I've always wanted to settle down with a Black king." She set the wine and glasses down on the coffee table and opened the blanket.

"And there's nothing wrong with that. What would be wrong is being so set in your ways that you don't enter all the doors God is opening for you."

"Speaking of—"

"No, we're not speaking of…did you hear what I said?"

"Loud and clear, but you should listen to your own advice. So, like I said, speaking of…are you going to let down your walls with Cheta?"

I snuggled with my sister under the blanket. The movie was all set. Picking up the remote, I turned to her.

"I don't know, Dee. If I'm being honest, I'm intrigued by him. He's one gorgeous man," I moaned. "The only reason I'm considering it is because he expressed interest in me before all this started. But is that the right thing to do? Can I handle what his life brings? If I let my walls down, I might fall for him. What if he wants out at the end? I'll be out here sick."

"What if he doesn't? You're over here conjuring up imaginary scenarios. Go with the flow."

"I don't even know what that is…" I brushed my hand over my face. "I'm so ashamed to say this, but I don't trust myself. If I—"

"Stop," she yelled. Her hair flew out of the loose bun she had it in. "I'm sorry, but stop. You let our parents do that to you. One mistake, Rei. I know I try to keep the peace, but one lousy mistake and they've made you second guess everything you do." She paused. "You don't know how proud I am of you that you stuck with your guns and started Body Glow. Despite their constant negativity and shade. Please, Sis, have the courage to do that with your personal life. The first step was getting rid of Martrell…" She wiped imaginary sweat from her brow.

I laughed at her dramatics.

"Sis, I was scared there for a minute. The Lord sure did hear my prayer when you got outta that train wreck."

Martrell Harris was the second son of Deacon and Mrs. Harris, longtime members of our church back home and close friends of my parents. He was a nice guy and good looking in his own right. According to my mother, he'd be perfect for me. At that time, I was living at home and would've done anything to get her off my back. So, I agreed when Martrell asked me out.

What started off as me fulfilling an obligation became a full-blown relationship. He wasn't bad, but he wasn't my type. There was zero passion between us. It didn't help that he was also pretty set in his patriarchal ways. He traveled a lot as a geologist, making me okay with an absentee boyfriend. Until suddenly, he proposed during one of his visits. He claimed he had a new job overseas and wanted me to go with him so we could raise our children. That knocked sense into me immediately.

"Promise me, you'll try to have fun. Don't lose yourself, but be open to the possibility. By the way, where's my in-law?"

I rolled my eyes at her. She'd been singing this in-law tune since last week. "Better stop saying that. He might not be your anything after this lunch we're supposed to be having with mom and dad." My parents had asked to see the "disrespectful man" who put a ring on my finger without going to see them first.

She shook her head. "Ha! Glad I'll be gone, but I trust Cheta can handle himself." She threw some popcorn in her mouth.

My eyes darted to the timer on the TV. Almost ten o clock. "He went out with one of his cousins and I think Zane."

"Check you out. That's right, sis, keep up with your man."

"You're silly. Play the movie."

Deja laughed and picked up the remote. She'd changed her mind about what she wanted to watch. I was down for whatever. As she scrolled through the options, I picked up my phone and went to Instagram. I went to my business page checking to see if I had any questions or DMs. I had two, which I quickly answered, then went to my personal page. Nothing much, but I had so many new followers. That was the norm on all my social media platforms all week.

Next, I found myself on Cheta's page. He'd posted a picture about an hour ago. Dressed in an all-black ensemble, he looked divine. The shirt he wore looked like silk and had the top button open, displaying two gold tennis chains. I warred with myself on whether I wanted to comment.

Deja must've noticed because she shoved me on the shoulder. "Go ahead."

"Hmm, I don't know…"

"Don't you see all those thirsty women in the comments?"

That reality irritated me, but instead of an actual comment, I used an emoji. Heart eyes. I set my phone down. We started *The Man From Toronto* with Kevin Hart and one other dude. We were laughing and having fun when my phone buzzed with a text.

Cheta: 'Preciate the hearts. I'll be by to get you by 9 a.m. Pack a bag. Tell Deja I said wassup.

Smiling I responded. **What's the magic word?**

Cheta: There are two actually…be ready

My smile widened. Setting the phone down, I returned my focus to the movie. I had no idea what Cheta had in mind for tomorrow. I hoped it didn't involve a bunch of cameras in our faces.

"I don't understand. How did you know?"

I walked around the red Sportsman 450 H.O. I knew the make and model of a Polaris ATV from anywhere. I was still shocked at how Cheta knew about my thrill for riding. With his arms folded against his broad chest, he smiled at me. I told him he didn't smile enough and now it seemed he always blessed me with his. It was a blessing because only his family got that side of him. He leaned against the black Sportsman 570. A short distance away, two other men were engaged in conversation next to an F150 with a landscape trailer attached to it.

"It's my job to know your pleasures, guilty or otherwise."

You see, words like those scrambled my mind. He'd been saying things like that all weekend. At first, I thought it was harmless flirting, but then something about the way he looked at me had me thinking there was some realness behind it. I felt his eyes on me as I inspected the ATV. True to his word, he arrived at my condo the previous morning. He and Deja clowned around for a bit before he took my overnight bag and ushered me out the door. I wasn't sure where we were going. All he said was, he knew I had a rough week, and he wasn't there like he wanted to be because he wanted to give me space. I wasn't sure what he meant because we talked almost every day. He clarified by saying he was trying to let me breathe, but also wanted me to know he was a phone call away.

We stopped for breakfast at one of the most popular breakfast spots in the city. At first, I was hesitant because of the crowd and picture I knew would follow. I remember Cheta cutting his brown eyes at me before demanding that I trust him. That I did and I didn't regret it. Whatever he did must have caused a fortune because we had a nice meal in complete privacy and were out of there without being noticed.

"This weekend is about you taking a breath. We can put on for the public another time," he'd said.

Once we were back on the road, he told me where we were going. That was after I attempted to find out if he was ticklish. I'd never initiated touch between us before. He was the one always grabbing my hand or trying to get a loose loc out of my face. When I reached over and touched him, we were both shocked, but spoke nothing of it. What I didn't expect was for him to squeal. I'd never heard a man, a very mannish one at that, squeal like a toddler from a tickle. After threatening my life if I told anyone, Cheta told me we were headed to his cabin in Blue

Ridge. It took us about ninety minutes to get to the serene mountain area in North Georgia.

We arrived at the three-bedroom, three bath cabin, and I was completely enamored with the rustic mixed with a little contemporary feel. The warm, spacious, wooden structure had two levels and was perched on a quiet, private hill above what Cheta called the Toccoa River. The cabin was surrounded by majestic pines like in those lifestyles for the rich and famous magazines. There was a fully functioning kitchen, a cozy living room with a fireplace, wrap-around deck, and a perfect view of the lake.

Cheta showed me to my room, and after making sure I was settled, he left. I had no idea what the weekend would bring, but he'd been the perfect gentleman. After a needed nap, we had a catered lunch by the lake, strolled to the flea market, and ended the evening with dinner, wine, and surprisingly… dancing.

In his arms, a calm I'd never experienced came over me. His palm rested on the small of my back while he drew me into his chest. The smell of his cologne kept me in an unknown euphoria. The warmth and comfort of being blanketed in his arms when he pulled me close was heaven. The gesture had me dreaming things I never dared to imagine would be possible for me.

All day, he'd done little things that made me all tingly inside. The way he caressed the back of my hand with his thumb, rubbed the back of my neck, intertwined our fingers, or pulled me close to him so he could plant a kiss on my temple or forehead. Our chemistry was off the charts. I knew this because the eyes didn't lie. His brown eyes told the secrets he held close.

The day was magical but despite all that, he never kissed me. He gave me enough to crave him, but pulled back before anything came of it. I went to bed flustered. I knew there was no law stating he had to kiss me first, but I was traditional like that and there was nothing wrong with that. I stayed up wondering why he'd do all that, but not kiss me.

I made up my mind to confront him in the morning. About

what exactly, I didn't know. Treating me like a lady? I knew I was tripping, but for months, he'd been after me. Now he had me in some capacity and was acting like he wanted to friend-zone me. Maybe the week he stayed away, he had someone with him? Either way, I could train my mind to handle it, but the casualness of his attitude was confusing.

I had it all mapped out in my head when I went to bed. I would deal with him in the morning.

Imagine my surprise when there was a light tap on my door in the early morning. It was Cheta telling me to get dressed, and that he had a surprise for me.

Once we got outside, the cool mountain air hit my face and I took a deep breath. Then my eyes bugged when I spotted two ATVs being rolled out of the F150.

"Stop playing with me," I said, running towards them. I came back to stand next to him when I was finally done with my inspection of the vehicles.

"How am I playing with you, Rei?" he asked.

I detected a smirk on his face, one I couldn't see clearly in the darkness of the early morning. I did feel when he started approaching me. I shifted my weight to one leg. I wished the guy who I assumed would be leading us down the trail would hurry up.

"Answer me," he demanded.

I appreciated his ability to balance between domination and surrender. However, his sexy dominance was becoming my addiction.

"Your casual lukewarm attitude. I can't take it. I need a clear mind."

He inclined his head to the side and pinned me with his stare. "I'm not exactly sure I know what you're talking about, but I think I have an idea. So listen, I need you to hear me when I say this because I'll say it only once." He paused, searching for my eyes.

When he had them, he continued. "Contract or not, nobody makes me do or behave in a way I don't want to. All you'll ever get from me is…me. Pretending takes too much work. Sure, I have an image to fix, but there was no way I was doing this with someone I didn't at least find very attractive and was enthralled by. This weekend is about you relaxing and us getting to know each other better." He chuckled. "I already know I can't stand your snoring."

I laughed. "I don't snore." According to him, on the drive over, I'd snored like I was aiming for an award.

"Shiiiiiddd. The most annoying part is you can't seem to pick a tempo. One minute, you're whispering, two seconds later, you're like a grizzly."

I threw my head back and cackled.

He shook his head and pointed at me. "We need to fix that. Don't make any sense."

"Hey, Nyce, you ready?" one of the men approaching us called out.

Cheta glanced at the guy, and then me, before his glare returned to the man. "You don't see my lady?"

The man thumbed his nose and smirked. "I ain't know if you wanted me to speak. You know how you get."

I turned to Cheta, curious about that statement. *Is this where he brings all his women?*

"Now, I ought to knock you out. See how she's looking at me?" He turned to me and draped his arm around my neck. "No, I've not brought anyone up here but you."

"My bad…I was referencing his temper. I'm Damian and I'll be your guide through the trails today." He stretched out his hand.

I took it in a handshake. "Nice to meet you. I'm Reign."

"Okay, that's enough," Cheta said, a frown marring his face. "D, gimme me a minute and we'll be ready."

Damian went to mount his ATV and Cheta turned to me. "*Asa*

m, I'm trying to introduce you to Cheta because Nyce is a lot to handle. Know this though, there's nothing lukewarm about me. My message will always be loud and clear. Like the one I'm about to give now."

Leaning in, Cheta cupped my face. A force I couldn't identify pulled me to the tip of my toes before he captured my lips. Yielding to pressure from the tip of his tongue, I opened my mouth. Shivering, I moaned, urging him on while enjoying a world of endless pleasure. Overcome by the desperate need to breathe, I shifted against him. Cheta broke off our contact, but followed it up with a series of quick pecks on my lips before grabbing my hand.

"Come on." He assisted me in mounting my all-terrain while talking smack. "After I've stalked your IG, interrogated Deja, rented these vehicles, and had them brought from the city… all to surprise you and you out here questioning me like I stole something."

Rolling my eyes at him, I secured myself and took the helmet from him. "That's sweet and I am surprised. Thank you."

He placed his hand over his heart and twisted his lips, showing his dissatisfaction. "I'm not feeling it. I have to feel it."

I tucked a loc behind my ear. "How?"

"Let me think on it. Meanwhile, I'm right behind you. Follow D. No stunts or I'm shutting it all down." He made his way to his vehicle.

I giggled. "Yes, sir."

He stopped mid-stride, turned, and lifted his brow. "Sir? *Asa*, you're playing with fire, baby."

Deciding not to respond, I closed the front of the helmet and started the engine. Call me crazy, but I was looking forward to meeting Nyce.

7

———

CHETA

Setting the glass of orange juice down, I rubbed my hands together as the waiter approached with our food. Reign giggled at my actions, but I waved her off. What I thought would be a quick surprise for her turned into her pleading to do another trail. By the time we got done with the first one, which was four miles long, my stomach was dragging on the floor.

Damian ignored all the signs I gave him and told her that he knew of another one that was two miles long. Pretty quickly, I'd come to learn that her eyes were my kryptonite. So, my pangs of hunger took a back seat to fulfilling her desire. When I woke up this morning, I didn't plan on riding back and forth for ten plus miles. The only person who could get me to do it was Reign freaking Davis.

"I'on know what you're laughing at. If I die, you gonna play out my contract?"

"Stop being dramatic. I don't know a lot, but I know that's not a thing in basketball."

The waiters started placing the plates on the table. Eggs, French toast, sausages, grits, toast, biscuits, fruit, and the steak I ordered. We'd been back to the cabin to get freshened up and were right back out.

I found this quaint bed and breakfast when I first came to Blue Ridge some time ago. Like I told Reign, I hadn't brought any other woman up here. This was where I came to chill when I didn't wanna be bothered with travel. The small town was a great escape from the city. The thing I could do without were the occasional stares of nervousness and curiosity. Probably folks trying to figure out what I was doing in a predominantly Caucasian town. That was their problem because this rich Black man was going to go wherever he wanted.

With our food set before us, I asked Reign what she wanted and fixed her plate. After handing over hers, I fixed mine.

"True, you couldn't even reach the basket if you wanted to." I loved her height. It allowed me to tower over her. I stayed clowning her about it.

"Says the man who's crying about riding a few miles."

"Yeah, whatever." I reached for her hand, and we said grace.

For the first few moments, we ate in semi-silence. When my eyes no longer crossed from hunger, I looked at Reign. Something I caught myself doing a lot. Staring at her. Not like a creep, but admiring and soaking her in. The glow of her skin wasn't only from her skin products. There was a certain light about her, one that I noticed she tried to reel in when she felt seen.

"What?" She frowned, wiping the sides of her mouth.

"Can't I admire you?"

"You're making me nervous." She lifted her coffee to her lips.

I looked over my shoulder in feigned agitation. "Nervous? Is there someone we should be running from?"

"Why can't you be serious?" She forked some eggs and pushed them in her mouth.

"But I am." Raising a brow I asked, "*Asa m?*"

Placing her elbow on the table, Reign cupped her cheek. "You keep calling me that. What does it mean?"

"*Asa* means beauty, beautiful…the *m* at the end emphasizes possession." I winked. "You're my beauty."

She dipped her chin for a moment before we locked eyes again. "Beauty isn't all it's cracked up to be."

"Why do you always do that?" I asked.

"Do what?"

"Have a counter to any compliment I give you. You know a simple 'thank you' will suffice. I congratulated you on moving to the final stage of the deal with Coleman, you blew it off. I complimented you on growing your business and going after your dreams, you blew it off. Why do you do that? You don't strike me as insecure, or am I reading you wrong?" The first time she did it, I ignored it, but it had become a pattern. I knew for a fact she wasn't afraid to speak her mind, so I wondered where the disconnect was.

"I'm sorry—"

"Don't apologize. I'm curious."

"I don't trust what this beauty attracts." She twirled one of her locs.

"Explain."

"It took a lot of work to get here." She shrugged. "Sometimes I can't let go of how people treated me before this beauty." She air quoted the word beauty. "Believe it or not, I had bad acne as a teenager, even as a young adult. High school was horrible for me."

"So, your venture into skincare was driven by your pain?"

She'd told me the "how" of her skincare journey, but we'd never discussed the "why." Reign was resilient. I kinda figured that out in NYC when she first told me about Coleman. Now, hearing how she got there made me respect her more.

"Deja has always been the beautiful one. I, on the other hand, was always 'her sister'."

Her laughter was dry, exposing her hidden pain. I coached myself on remaining silent, letting her get it out.

"She was a cheerleader, ran track, and was in every club you could think of. While I…I was riddled with acne and made fun of, which caused me to hide from the world. I've never been jealous of my sister, but being defined by her and my skin problems shattered my confidence." Reign looked right through me, although I knew her memory of the past was what she saw.

"After a few years, I finally found something that helped clear my skin." She took another sip of coffee. "But something was always lacking. The fragrance, the consistency, the preservatives. So, I decided to develop my own line. From pain… and passion of course, Body Glow was born. Besides, I studied chemistry." She shrugged. "I don't mean to brush off compliments, but sometimes—"

"You don't know what's real and what's not?" I finished for her. My mind traveled to my sisters and how they switched up once I became a celeb with my own money.

"Yes! In my final year of high school, I did a stupid thing. Very stupid—"

"You gonna tell me what that was?"

"Maybe someday…"

I searched my memory, trying to bring the background check Amara had done on her to the forefront of my mind. There was nothing in there that was concerning. Whatever she was talking about couldn't be that bad. So, I settled for her response.

"I'mma hold you to that."

"Since then, my parents have treated me like I was the biggest disappointment known to mankind. I guess moving back home after college to save money to pursue a pipe dream didn't help." She raised her index finger. "But then, after several months of taking care of my skin and diet, the beauty came."

Her disdain for the word was visceral.

"Suddenly, my mom wanted to show me off. That's when she introduced me to her friend's son. Something that wouldn't have happened if I wasn't now considered beautiful."

I adjusted myself in my seat, curious as to where this story was going. If she was about to tell me she was in a situationship, these people might ban me from this restaurant.

"You can set your shoulders down. I haven't talked to him in years." She rolled her eyes.

That was another thing that had me looking at her in awe. Somehow, she had the uncanny ability to know what I was thinking. None of it I'd ever confirm, but she was spot on most of the time.

"After years of struggling with my esteem, I was ready to do anything that would appease her. I ignored all the red flags with Martrell. Years of rejection turned me into a 'pick me.'"

I allowed her words to sink in. A few beats passed between us, then I took her hands. My words were halted by the waiter that walked over. We expressed our gratitude for her stellar service while she cleared the empty plates. Once we were alone, I reached across the table and took Reign's hands in mine again. She lowered her eyes. I didn't like that.

"Look at me. No matter what you did *then*, what you did *next* is the only thing that matters. You could've wallowed, given up on life, or been bitter, but you did none of that. You pushed ahead. Believe me, I feel you. I know what it's like to question who's really for you. Hear me when I say this, you'll always be safe with me. The moment I feel I can't protect and provide you peace...we'll have a conversation."

She smiled and tugged my beard. "I'm sure trust is a problem for all celebrities."

"I don't know about that. For me, the women in my life are the ones who have me second-guessing a lot." For the next few minutes, I told her about the relationship between me and my sisters. I also told her the reason and the role my parent's played. We both laughed and agreed our parents weren't ideal, but again who was?

"I'm so sorry to hear that. When you told me about your mistrust of women, I'd imagined it stemmed from a relationship."

"Well, that too. Let's say when I had my accident, my ex decided my best friend's shoulder was the best one to cry on. His shoulder somehow became his bed, and the rest is history."

"That's awful. You don't have to be so cavalier about it. Wow, that must've hurt."

"It did and I'm not. But it's old news. Doesn't sting anymore." Pausing, I checked my phone to see if I had any missed calls from my cousins. They knew I was off the grid but even at that, I never shut down on them completely. We had to head back to Atlanta, but there was one more place I wanted to take her to. "You ready to go?"

Reign smiled at me. "I see you shutting down, but first, I also want you to know, you'll always be safe with me."

Her eyes remained on me, forcing me to digest the same words I'd used for her. We both struggled with trust, but for different reasons. I prayed that helped us handle each other differently. I really liked Reign and the thought of hurting her made my chest tight.

"Please behave yourself."

"Amara, I'm not a child."

"I know. A child will fear the consequences of going against the grain. You sir, simply don't care." Amara let out a heavy sigh and walked toward my kitchen.

I laughed at the analogy she was using to handle me. As expected, a lot of news outlets asked for an interview with me and my "fiancée." Most of which I'd asked Amara to decline without hesitation. However, Reign and I would be leaving for Enugu next weekend, and I wanted to get this last, "necessary" to-do out of the way. Hopefully, with this interview, folks could go back to minding their business. Blue Ridge was a welcome getaway, but we eventually returned to reality.

When I dropped Reign off last Sunday, that reality came crashing down, hard. I spotted two cameras flashing outside her apartment. As though that wasn't enough, they started screaming our names. I knew that if I didn't give them a photo opportunity, they'd only get more aggressive. Because she'd been asleep during the ride, Reign complained about not looking right for a picture. She looked beautiful, but I never wanted her uncomfortable, so I pulled her into me. If they couldn't take a picture with her face in my chest, then they were fresh outta luck.

After signing autographs and taking a few pictures, we chilled at her house a bit before I called Izaak over. I wondered how they knew about our movements. That question was quickly answered when I saw our picture circulating. Someone took a photo from the gift shop I'd taken her to after breakfast and posted it.

The now familiar, soft, warm, floral fragrance floated through the air. Reign had arrived. Instead of a studio, the decision was made to give the interview from my home in Atlanta. I made my way to the front of the house to greet her. This wasn't her first time here, so she knew her way around. Three nights ago, we had dinner prepared by my chef. I had given her the tour of my eight-bedroom, nine-bathroom home.

Since our first kiss, that was the first thing I always wanted to do when I saw her. But that night, she wouldn't stop talking about my two living rooms, game/theater room, state-of-the-art kitchen and large pool located in the massive backyard. This time, I didn't have that problem. She glanced up and smiled when she felt my presence. She dropped her keys in her bag, and placed it on the table. Before she could get a word out, I pulled her to me, capturing her lips in a breathless exchange bridled with passion.

"Someone's happy to see me," she teased.

"Hmm… you a'ight." My lips hovered over hers.

She swatted my arm, and I doubled over in pretend hurt. "Woman, those tiny hands hurt." I ushered her further into the house. "How was work?"

She waved at the crew setting up the cameras as we passed them by. "The usual. Busy, busy."

Reign shared that her business had picked up tremendously since the engagement announcement. Also, with the way things were going with Coleman, she was going to need a bigger warehouse space. Although she didn't need my help yet, I let her know it was there whenever she did need it.

"Have you had anything to eat? You need some time to freshen up?"

Reign paused, forcing me to halt. She stepped in front of me placing her hand on my chest. Serenity washed over me as I stared down at her.

"Calm down. Everything will be fine," she said.

I grunted and kissed her forehead.

She grinned up at me. "Why do you hate the press so much?"

"I don't hate them. I dislike them. All they're concerned about is views, clicks, and ratings. They forget that there are real people behind their misleading headlines."

She cupped my cheek. "That's their job. As long as you know who you are, don't worry about them."

I placed my hand over hers and leaned into her touch. "And I don't—"

"You did kinda give them material."

I removed her hand from my face. "See you were almost making sense. Besides, that was years ago. That's the problem. They're trying to keep me where they met me. I'm so glad God is not a man, 'cause humans will always human. Whose side are you on anyway?"

"Yours baby. Always yours. Now let's get this over with."

This was the first time she'd called me anything other than

Cheta. I wasn't sure if it was because of the audience we had, or if she truly meant it. I'd leave it alone for now.

"You better be." I brushed my lips against hers.

About thirty-five minutes later, I was outside on the covered patio, sitting opposite Layla Assan. She was one of the most respected Black voices in the lifestyles of the rich and famous. The format of the interview was a solo segment first, then Reign would join me for the second half after which we'd do some rapid-fire questions. Currently, Reign and Amara were outside the frame.

"We've covered your global ambassadorship for BAL, projects you're doing beyond the NBA, your new contract with the Harriers and what you anticipate for the upcoming season. By the way, we're holding you to that championship promise." Layla leaned in. "Now that we got all that out of the way, let's get down to the juicy stuff."

Although I didn't particularly love to, I could talk business all day. My personal life on the other hand, I hated talking about. I rolled my shoulders and adjusted my position in anticipation. I knew how these things went. The fans didn't only want to know Nyce. They also wanted to know Cheta.

"Your cousin got engaged some time ago and I remember you saying…" She looked down at her note card.

I trained my expression to conceal my thoughts on what I knew she was about to say.

"Quote, 'Congrats my people. Y'all don't get any ideas. That won't be me for many years to come, but I love this for my people.' End quote." She looked up at me.

"Is there a question there?"

"Umm, yes. If that was you not too long ago, you can understand why the public is split down the middle on whether your engagement is real or whether it's for publicity?"

"I appreciate the public's need to know about the *validity* of *my* engagement, however, that's between my wife-to-be and me.

I'll say this though, Reign is very private. We met some time ago. Immediately I laid eyes on her, I knew I had to know more. Don't believe the stories that a man can't decide. When a man knows, he knows. The proof of desire is in the pursuit.

"With me being who I am, we wanted to get to know each other in private and that's what we did. Unfortunately for us, the public got wind of it before we were ready." I clarified the best I could without telling a lie. They didn't need to know the actual sequence of events.

Layla raised her brow. I knew she wasn't convinced, but that was her problem. "I and I'm sure a number of our viewers find it strange that with the amount of time you spend in the tabloids…" She glanced down at her notecard.

I sat back as she began a run-down of the unfavorable things I'd done. Bar fights, my very public breakup, random women who'd taken pictures of me while I slept, the recent pregnancy debacle and lawsuits. Some suits were against me personally or because of something someone on my team did. Except for the pregnancy thing, everything she'd listed was five plus years old. This was a prime example of the press not letting me be great.

"With all of that, you've had a girlfriend who turned into a fiancée, and no one knew."

I crossed my leg over my knee. "I don't know what to tell you. It is what it is. Besides, all those things you ran down are all old news." I scooted to the edge of my chair, ready to bring this thing to an end.

"As a matter of fact, where's your camera?" I pointed at the two cameras I saw, wondering which one I could speak directly into.

I could feel Amara's eyes on me. She was just gonna have to be upset. Layla's eyes danced around—her apprehension palpable. She, like others, wondered what was about to happen. She pointed to the camera. I turned my focus to it. Rolling my tongue across my teeth, I cleared my throat.

"Listen up. I love the game of basketball. I'm honored to play for my city. I can take anything you throw at me because mainly, I ignore y'all." I chuckled. "My lady isn't a secret, but she's private. There's a difference. Now, this is my personal appeal to y'all. Leave her alone. She bothers no one and doesn't deserve to be hounded simply because she's attached to me. When she's happy, I'm at peace. When I'm at peace, I play better...y'all get where I'm going with this? Appreciate your understanding." I leaned back into my chair. I was done addressing this.

"Wow. Ladies and gents, Cheta 'Nyce' Kalu has spoken. We'll be right back to see how well this couple knows each other."

The producer yelled, "Cut."

I stood, took off my mic and walked toward Reign. Amara met me, but I raised my hand, halting her rant. I reached for Reign and pulled her close. She hadn't said anything, but I felt her nervous energy.

"If you're coming to yell at me, too bad. I'm not apologizing."

Amara rolled her eyes. "And I wasn't going to ask you to. What you did wasn't part of the plan, and that was Layla Assan you were talking to. However, it was so believable." Amara's eyes darted between Reign and me. "Is there something you two need to tell me?"

"No," I answered and pulled Reign to the corner for some privacy. I looked into her eyes. "You good?"

She nodded. "I see Nyce reappeared."

I dismissed her reference to the disaster of a dinner we had with her parents. That was also the day Reign and I had our first real fight. The way they talked to her had my insides boiling. It wasn't outright disrespect, but underhanded shade. Then insinuating I was no good and wanted to use her had me about to explode. But for my woman's sake, I gritted my teeth and took it.

But when her mother said, "I see you still can't think for yourself," I lost it. Reign pleaded with me to let it go, but I couldn't. I read them for filth, and as expected, they asked me to leave their home. But not before predicting Reign would be back with tears in her eyes. I was raised to give respect to those older than me. Now though, I was learning to give respect only when earned. I didn't care if you knew Moses personally.

"I'm nice on the court and nice with delivering a good read."

There was a pregnant pause. She lowered her eyes briefly, then lifted them to mine. "Thank you. No one has stood up for me like that before."

"Don't ever thank me for protecting your mental." I tapped my finger against her temple. "Your emotions." I touched the center of her chest. Her breath hitched. "Or your body."

I placed both hands on her waist and drew her closer. Our bodies were flush while our eyes remained locked in a heart-pounding gaze. This woman had me acting so out of the norm that I couldn't recognize myself most days. How the tides changed. This was the same thing I clowned Arinze for doing. The burning desire to taste her had me leaning in.

"Okay, we're back on in two minutes," the producer yelled.

"We'll finish this later," I whispered against her lips.

"I'm counting on it."

Several minutes later, Layla clapped. "Both of you are eight for eight."

Reign and I were on the sofa opposite her. When we first got back from the commercial break, Reign introduced herself to the world. She talked about her school, and her business. She didn't mention her parents by name, but briefly talked about growing up in Savanah. I admired her boss up when Layla tried to trip her up on occasion. Her finger tightened around mine, showing her unease. It took everything in me not to speak. I never wanted her on camera in the first place.

But Reign held her own. It was a beautiful thing to watch. We were in a room full of people, but we sat comfortably as though we were watching one of those animes she loved so much. Reign had one leg on my lap while my hand idly massaged her ankle.

We'd answered questions like full name, favorite movies, food, color, secret talent, and our anger language. Now that was a first, but I learned it after we argued when leaving her parents' home. Reign needed space while I wanted to talk quickly and squash the beef.

"Okay, last two questions. Your favorite morning drink?" Layla asked.

"On a light day at work, she has a Thai cold coffee. On days when she's gonna work late, she has some strong nasty coffee that could probably show up on a drug test," I answered.

The room erupted in laughter at my comment. Reign rolled her eyes because I told her that a few days ago when I called myself taking a quick sip from her morning coffee. I quickly spit it all over the floor.

"I can't believe you said that. Anyway, he drinks these kale smoothies. It's mixed with banana, blueberries, yogurt, and cinnamon." She made a stank face. "It couldn't be me."

"I have to say, I didn't expect you two to be so much fun together. Okay, last question. Cheta, what's Reign's long-term goal? Reign, same question."

I pinned Reign with my gaze. "To increase brand awareness and recognition for Body Glow Essentials across America. She wants to help women all over the country realize their...beauty." I paused and swept my eyes across her face. "Their true beauty." Noticing her tear up, I squeezed her ankle. I might not act like I listened, but I heard and retained everything she told me.

Reign dabbed the corner of her eye with her finger. "Man." She fanned her face with her hand. "His is to be a conduit for talented boys and girls to have a similar professional basketball career without having to leave Africa if they don't want to."

I leaned over and kissed Reign's cheek. She understood me.

"Beautiful, so beautiful. There you have it people. Oh, one more question, from me of course. When's the big day?"

"When we're ready to make it public, you'll be our first call," Reign said.

Layla turned to the camera. "The Missus has spoken. Thank you for watching this special exclusive with Cheta Kalu and Reign Davis. I'm Layla Assan. Good night."

Soon after, everyone was packed up and gone. Amara was on the last flight to Dallas, her home base. Her clients knew that her husband, Ejike, only let her out of his sight for so long before he was on a plane to be with her. I clowned him once, especially since they had a son who was already in college. He told me then that when my time came, I'd understand.

My eyes followed Reign as she made her way to the kitchen to warm up our dinner. We had no real formal title to what we had going on, but the unfamiliar twinge in my heart made clear exactly what he'd been trying to tell me.

8

REIGN

So, that man has you not calling your mother?

I glanced at my mother's text and set the phone down on the nightstand. It'd been exactly five weeks since I'd gotten fake engaged and two days since I'd been in Enugu, Nigeria. Returning my focus to my open suitcase on the bed, I secured the light robe around my freshly showered body. Finally deciding on my attire for the day, I laid my clothes out.

Cheta was scheduled to handle some business with Jidenna, while Ifunanya, his cousin, was on her way to the house to take me around town. Cheta, I, Jidenna, and his cutie of a daughter had arrived late in the evening. Jasmine and Arinze wouldn't make it until the following week. The day after we'd arrived was a complete blur for me. I knew it would happen, but the time difference and jet lag for real had me moving around like a zombie. Cheta teased me so bad, but he also made sure I was comfortable.

This wasn't my first time in Africa though. In my senior year, AP Geography class, we were given the option to go to Egypt or Greece. I chose Egypt. That was so long ago. Although I kept up with the continent in some capacity, I wasn't overly invested in it.

Now I was back here as an adult—an adult who was pretending to be the fiancée of a national treasure.

Cheta told me that soccer was more prevalent here, but when we landed, there was no mistaking that everyone knew exactly who he was. The only difference between his celebrity here and the US was that folks didn't seem too bothered. After a picture and an autograph, they kept it moving. It reminded me of that Bible verse, a prophet is not honored in his hometown.

Once again, I took in the room I was in. I thought his house in Atlanta was gorgeous, but it had nothing on this one. The fact that he built it without a mortgage gave me a clearer vision of how deep his pockets were. The opulence of the Kalu compound showed that his family wasn't something to play with. It was like something straight out of Beverly Hills. There was about a five-minute drive from the heavily guarded gate to where the houses started. His uncles, parents, grandparents and cousins all had nice sized houses in the Kalu estate.

Slipping into my orange, off-shoulder halter dress, I turned to my phone that buzzed again, reminding me of the text I received earlier. I did text my mother along with the rest of my family in our family chat. She was looking for something to say I did to her. For someone who said I was no longer her child, she really was invested in my every move. I knew she was angry and didn't mean it. Her real problem was that I wasn't towing the line.

I rolled my eyes, picked up the phone and responded to her. Ignoring her comment, I instead decided to let her know how I was. Which was great.

To my parents, and to be honest, a good majority of the public, Cheta was a talented troublemaker who was arrogant and reckless with a quick temper. Quite honestly, I'd believed the same, but the man I now knew was far from that. Sure, he had the temper and a confidence that bordered on arrogance, but he was none of those things with me. Once I decided to open my mind, I understood why he was so misjudged. Cheta really didn't care what people who weren't in his inner circle thought. According to him, a "care" had to be earned before he gave one.

I giggled when I remembered that conversation. That man was really a handful. Rummaging through my makeup bag, I prayed I packed my Fenty gloss. Although I had known I'd be coming here a while ago, I'd been so busy that I barely had time to prepare. Luckily, Ebonie was able to get two weeks off work, so she could be at the store full time. I owed my girl big because I know for a fact this wasn't what she planned for her vacation.

I'd done my final presentation with Coleman, who were supposed to decide in the coming days. I had my laptop with me because I also had other things to do and couldn't shut my business down for two whole weeks.

There was a light knock on the door. Glancing over my appearance, I asked the person to come in. One of Cheta's domestic staff peeked her head through the door.

"Madam, good morning. Aunty Ifunanya is downstairs."

"Good morning, thank you. Please call me Reign and tell her I'll be right down."

A small smile crept up the lady's face before she left the room. She did that the first time she told me she couldn't call me by my first name. Cheta asked me to go with it for her comfort, but it still felt weird. He explained her calling me "Madam" was a sign of respect and not that she thought I was old. Jasmine had given me a heads up of what to expect. But to experience it for myself was surreal. Being the majority race, seeing the opulence of some areas and the utter poverty in others. Nigeria had a lot of things and was a beautiful place, but Cheta explained that if the government wasn't failing its people, the country could be so much more.

Checking myself out again in the mirror, I slipped my feet into a pair of black sandals, picked up my leather crossbody and left the room.

"Madam, don't you look cute." Ifunanya glanced my way

before returning to her current mission—surfing through channels on the gigantic television in the living room.

My smile dropped. "Not you too…"

She waved me off. "Relax. The context of my 'madam' and the staff's 'madam' are two different things. Mine is like you saying… what do y'all say again? Yeah…sis…"

I shook my head at her. There was no doubt in my mind that the reason she and Cheta were so close was because they were the same in temperament and their reckless tongue. I liked her although our first meeting was a disaster.

Cheta had been over at my house. We'd had dinner and were playing Scrabble. I was winning, but he claimed I was cheating. Both of us were very competitive, so the tension was high. His phone rang and without saying anything, he answered. When a woman's voice with a Nigerian accent came through the speaker, I flipped. I'd heard of these immigrants and their secret wives back home. The fact that he was speaking in his native tongue further pissed me off.

He thought it was funny that I was going off in the background. When she asked him why he dropped an unfaithful woman only to get engaged to a deranged one, I took the phone from him. I still shuddered at how our conversation had started. After a harsh "Who is this?" from me, she hissed.

"Before you even start, don't. I'm his cousin, so I'd advise you to abort the mission." Then a moment later, she continued. "I like you though. You're not afraid to put him in his place." Ice laced her tone, but she was calm.

I was horrified. Cheta had told me about her, but in that moment, I couldn't see straight. I apologized to her, but of course, they both still teased me. Hence the "relax."

"Your man said he'll meet us for an early dinner, right?"

I nodded and glanced down at my phone. It was almost noon. The last message I got from Cheta was about an hour ago, asking if I was good and whether Ifunanya had arrived.

"Great. We'll stop at the tailor so I can pick up Jasmine's clothes for next weekend. Then you'll get measured for yours. After that, consider me your tour guide."

"I'm excited—" I stopped talking , caught off guard by the voices we could hear approaching.

"What do we even know about her?"

"There's no telling why he got engaged to her so quick."

"Ha! Do you think she has something on him? Or does she need something from him?"

"Maybe… you know he's always been a troublemaker, but Papa never sees it."

Ifunanya and I stood stunned while Cheta's sisters made their way down the hall. Or rather, I was stunned. Ifunanya rolled her eyes. The day before, despite my jet lagged state, I was briefly introduced to the Kalu clan. After a few minutes with them, I could tell how tight they were, but could also see they had dysfunction like any other family.

Arinze nailed it when he said Cheta was their grandmother's favorite. He had the matriarch of the family wrapped around his finger. His grandfather, uncles and aunties saw right through his smooth talk and finesse. His father was very proud of him, but his sisters and mother were exactly as he described them. While his sisters shot daggers at me all day, his mother towed the fine line between appeasing her daughters and not annoying her son. She wasn't mean or disrespectful, but she wasn't nice either. Cheta's mother was totally different from Jasmine's description of Arinze's.

Entering the living room, I watched as both their eyes bugged at seeing us standing there. Ifunanya sucked her teeth and pulled me by the arm.

"Ifunanya, you can't greet? What has gotten into you?" one of the sisters asked.

"No, I can't. And probably the same thing that has gotten into you, talking about someone who has done nothing to you."

"*O we ife ne me gi nisi?*"

"No, I'm not crazy, but you two—"

"Sister, leave her. No man will want her with this her attitude. Because she follows Cheta around, she thinks she's a man," the younger sister said.

I watched in dismay as Ifunanya laughed. Her sound lacked humor, but was more menacing. "Marriage isn't a life goal. Both of you are married. Explain to me how it has benefitted you? See, shift *o*, because if I descend on both of you, I'll be summoned by mama and papa."

"*Abeg o*. We were only saying the truth," the older sister doubled down.

"Whose truth? Reign, let's go leave these—"

I shook my head. My mind traveled back to all those times I let people bully me because I didn't fit some standard. I was too short. I was too smart to be Black. I wasn't pretty like my sister. I knew that to remain on their brother's good side, his sisters had to be nice to me. But that would be only when he was around. But I had to nip the disrespect in the bud. They didn't have to like me, but they had to watch their mouths.

"Look, I don't know what your beef is, but I'm gonna keep it classy. What's between your brother and I is just that...between us. But let's get one thing clear, I don't *need* anything from Cheta. However, what I *want* from him, money can't buy. So, your cash reservoir is safe."

"And that's on *periodt.*" Ifunanya yelled. Then she turned to me and whispered. "That's how you say it, *innit?*"

The atmosphere didn't call for it, but I chuckled as she dragged me toward the front door. Leaving the sisters to pick their faces off the floor.

"You're something else," I said, entering the back seat of the black, tinted G Wagon.

"It's my talent." Ifunanya winked at me and got in beside me.

The driver pulled off and we were on our way. I was super excited to see where Cheta grew up.

~

Home

A place or feeling of belonging. I took in a deep breath and allowed myself to bask in the fresh air from the Milliken hills. According to Cheta, the hills were about one hundred feet above sea level. We'd just finished a very romantic dinner in one of Enugu's high end restaurants. In the past four days since we'd been in Enugu, we'd had one big meal with the family, but had gone out to eat every night since then.

It had been three days since the run-in with his sisters and everything had been quite calm since then. That day, before we could even leave the estate good, a livid Cheta was calling my phone. I wondered how he knew, but Ifunanya later told me that the domestic staff must've snitched. After getting him to calm it down, we continued with our day.

At the tailor's, Ifunanya assisted me in picking out two traditional styles. She then briefly video called Jasmine for approval to make some changes to her own dress. Once we left there, we headed to Kalu International Inc. After obtaining her masters in England, Ifunanya moved back home to work for the family. She gave me a tour of the massive grounds and what I saw was like nothing I could've imagined.

The structure was the equivalent of a Fortune 500 company in the United States. The organization consisted of three, ten-story buildings, one for each pillar of the business. Each of the older Kalu men ran a division. The place was complete with a cafeteria, gym, staff and executive offices, library, and training spaces. The warehouses and factories were on another side of town, but we ran out of time before having to meet Jidenna and Cheta for an early dinner.

Since then, Cheta and I had spent almost every moment together. We'd visit with the family a little, then we'd be off to see the town. Golfing, forest tours, cave excursions or chilling by what was called the sand beach. There was something different every day, but the day always ended with food. Cheta was committed to taking me to a different restaurant every night. The cuisine varied from foods I could find in America to local dishes. It was awesome. Obviously, I liked some more than others, but what I hadn't been able to get used to was the amount of spice used in preparing the local dishes.

Currently, instead of heading back to the estate, Cheta decided to take me on a ride. I was enjoying the scenic view of the town. The vibes in the car were chill and conversation great as we enjoyed some mellow tunes. I was totally at...home.

Until I realized he was driving up this winding road. The road was like those freakishly dangerous roads in those *Fast & Furious* movies. The meandering terrain and deep gullies made me feel like I was on a natural rollercoaster. No matter how many times he told me to relax, my heart was in my throat until we got to the top. The view though...let's say it was kinda worth it. The slanting rays of the setting sun against the panoramic view of the city's metropolis was a thing of beauty. Beauty was too simple of a word to describe it. However, I'd go with it for now.

The warm orange tinge of the sky provided the perfect backdrop for reflecting on the last couple of days. I basked in the comfort of the tattooed arms around my waist and the broad chest that provided rest for my back. The outer serenity of the palpable silence we were enjoying was a direct contradiction to my inner battle. My mind raced at the realization that here, right now, in this position was where I felt like... home. A chill ran up my spine as my scrambled brain struggled to make sense of how Cheta had become my most thrilling adventure and place of belonging.

Home.

"You're so much more than how people portray you. Why don't you ever clear the air?" I asked the question that had been on my mind ever since we'd been in Enugu. A question that burned to be answered more after we toured his foundation earlier.

The CK Foundation had two major initiatives. One partnered with the NBA Africa Academy, sponsoring two kids a year through the Academy located in Senegal up to college graduation. The other initiative was a new vocational school.

"I never saw the need. In the beginning, it bothered me—"

"Because you did provide them content." I screamed when he tickled me.

"What did I tell you about being loyal to your man?"

"Stop! You're going to make me pee on myself."

"If you do, I'll clown you for the rest of your days." He leaned in an nipped my earlobe with his teeth.

His cool breath and beard against my neck caused my body to shudder. This man had perfected the art of taking my body to the edge and pulling back just in time to avoid us complicating things.

"Answer my question."

I felt him shrug. "I guess I've never cared enough. Still don't, but now I realize that my reputation influences not only the things I'm trying to do for myself, but my family, those who work for me and those I'm trying to help. My goal isn't to clear up their misconceptions." He took a breath. "I'm okay with who I am, and it'll never be up for negotiation to fit into anyone's expectation."

With his spiel, a realization hit me like a boulder. "So, you did this for me?"

"Did what for you?"

I shifted a little. I was still encased in his arms, but I could now see his face. "Don't be smug. This arrangement. You did it for me."

His eyes stared deep into mine before he captured my lips.

That was my confirmation. I knew he had something at stake too, but he'd been navigating everything just fine. Despite my present state of euphoria, my mind journeyed back to the day we made the agreement. He didn't agree to it until I told him about Coleman.

"Thank you."

"I wasn't completely selfless."

I frowned up at him.

"Don't look surprised. I'd been trying to get you to talk to me for months."

I laughed at his feigned despair. "I did talk to you."

He shook his head. "Nah, talking to me with a stank face don't count."

"I wasn't that bad. But if I was, which is a big if, I had reason to be."

"No, you didn't. You judged me based on what the internet told you."

"I'd give you that."

"I should sue you for pain and suffering."

I rolled my eyes. "Anyway, I wish I had had your outlook toward other people's opinions. It would've saved me a lot of stress."

For a large part of my life, I'd had to conform to belong. Once I didn't meet the standard or faltered in any way, the false sense of security I'd attained was quickly stripped from me.

As a teen, I was sentenced to six months in juvenile detention, thereby causing me to lose my scholarship. I was quickly stripped of belonging to my family. I had yet to share this with Cheta. I knew his people did a background check on me, but my record was sealed, so I knew they wouldn't find anything.

My parents had to dip into their savings and retirement accounts to send me to school. Something they resented doing till this day. That whole ordeal singlehandedly changed my relationship with my parents. Although they claimed they forgave me, they never really did.

When I didn't let Martrell convince me to move to a foreign country and become his baby making machine, I was also stripped of my sense of belonging in my church. How could I turn down the deacon's son? The opinion was that he was doing me a favor by marrying me. When I refused for my former boss to take credit for a formula I came up with, I was quickly stripped of the sense of belonging at work.

It took a while, with therapy, Ebonie screaming from the top of her lungs for me to get a grip, and me working on my relationship with Jesus, for me to finally accept Reign…me. Imperfection, mistakes and all, I still was worthy. My identity in Christ made me worthy.

Despite that knowledge, being brave and authentic wasn't always easy for me. Some days, I had it and some days I needed extra help. My current inner battle was fueled by the fact that for the month and a half I'd been with Cheta, I hadn't needed help. When we got back from Blue Ridge, there was an unspoken shift between us.

"You can't change the past. Focus that energy on building the future," he whispered.

"I'm trying to do that. Sometimes it gets overwhelming."

"I'll help you take the load off."

"As tempting as that is, all good things must come to an end."

"Says who?"

"Says our contract."

"Please tell me that you know, or at least I've shown you that what's between us is more than what's in that piece of paper." He brought my knuckles to his lips. "*Asa m*, I know you hear me."

I didn't know how he expected me to speak as he planted light kisses up my arm. Pleasure ripped through my body as his teasing traveled to my shoulder, the crook of my neck and was now settled at the back of my ear. A moan escaped my lips, causing him to chuckle. I lifted my arm and snaked it around his neck. The pads of my finger and my nails caressed and grazed his nape.

His teeth tugged my earlobe. "Answer me."

"Yes, you have shown me... something," I whispered. "But I'mma need you to clarify."

His smoldering gaze held me captive. "You're mine. Is that clear enough for you?"

"I don't know. I might need further explanation," I teased.

"How about I show you instead?"

Cheta didn't wait for an answer before he kissed my forehead, then my nose before he captured my lips, embarking on a soul snatching mission.

9

CHETA

From my leaning position against the rail of the balcony outside my bedroom, I watched Reign and my dad walk around the grounds. For the past week, I had deliberately hoarded her from my family. I wasn't ashamed of them, even my sisters who tried me. I loved them. The way I saw it, every family had some dysfunction. In fact, that was one of the things my baby and I shared.

My reason was as simple as my need to always have her close to me. I winced when I remembered that going back to the States, that wouldn't be as possible with the season starting and her getting deep into her business with Coleman. Who, by the way, gave my baby her due. She didn't get all their locations in the US, but they decided to start her off with their locations in the southern part of the country. That was twenty locations.

I didn't tell her, but I had made up my mind to get my business manager to make a personal call to Monica Coleman-Hunt if they didn't give Reign a call soon. After the initial debacle with the press, they told her they'd contact her, but then they started dragging their feet. That didn't sit well with me. I was giving them one more week, then I would've reached out.

I knew Reign would be mad at me, but I had warned her. She was attached to me now. Those close to me knew that I played about a lot, but my family, game, money and those I cared about would never be among those things. I cared about Reign, so she was going to have to deal. I was glad it didn't come to that because I preferred her happy.

I lifted my black *jalabiya* and slipped my feet into my slides. In the cool morning air, I strolled to the seat in the corner. I sat in a position where I could still see my folks and handle business at the same time.

Reign and I had barely finished breakfast when my dad arrived. We talked a bit about the chieftaincy conferment slated for next Wednesday. After Reign got the email from Coleman late last evening, we opened a glass of wine to celebrate.

However, I had a surprise for her. I had contacted the family pilot to get the plane ready. During one of our many conversations, Reign went on and on about shea butter. I knew that Arinze's cousins on his mother's side, the Adeshinas, had one of the biggest shea farms in Nigeria. I also knew that they not only grew shea for export, but they had started producing some shea butter.

To celebrate Reign, I was planning to surprise her with a tour of their facility. It was Friday, and we'd arrive later that night, tour the next day and be back before Nze and Jasmine arrived on Monday. I picked up my phone. Once we returned from Ibadan, everything would move so fast, that I needed to handle some business before we left. My mental rundown of my to-do list was interrupted when my phone rang.

"Hey 'Sim, *how far?*" I asked, once I answered the call from Qasim Adeshina.

"*I dey.* This one you called late last night…wassup?"

The concern in his voice made me smile. As I said before, we were connected through Arinze, so although we got along fine, we really didn't connect outside Nze.

"Yeah, everything's cool. I need a favor. Are you in Naija?"

"Nah, but wassup?"

I briefed him on what I needed. After teasing me about doing all this for a woman, he asked me to hold on. Weeks ago, he'd sent me a congratulatory text on my engagement, after which he proceeded to clown me for getting engaged after talking so much crap during Arinze's time. Since the only people that knew about the real situation were Arinze, Jasmine and Jidenna, I had to take his reckless mouth.

"Anyways, congrats again, man. Since I'm not there, I'll call Qasif. He should be able to arrange something before you guys land."

Qasif was his younger brother. The fact that their father gave all four of his sons names that began with the letter Q often made it hard to keep up with who was who.

"Thanks. I owe you one."

"Nah, you don't. We're family. Enjoy."

Once we disconnected the call, I peeped over the railing. Reign and my dad were now joined by my mother. She and my grandmother had already started doing too much since Arinze got engaged. They now had their sights set on me. For some reason, my mom always thought she had to compete with Arinze's mom, Aunty Bisi. I didn't even know why.

Nah, I take that back. I think that's something my dad caused when he started comparing her to his brother's wife when she hadn't given him a boy yet. Something I still couldn't wrap my head around, being that she could only grow what he gave her.

Despite all they'd been through, my parents' marriage seemed to work for them, so I didn't sweat it that much. Besides, my dad knew I'd never be alive and watch him mistreat my mother.

Anyway, when Reign and I arrived, she was met with the same skepticism as Jasmine. I could say it took a little more to convince them that we were good, being that I introduced her as my fiancée. It was unrealistic to expect the women in my life to take to Reign right away. What was important to me was that they respected her and treated her with kindness.

Everyone seemed to get it except my sisters. Real quick, I nipped whatever right they thought they had, coming to my house and questioning my girl, at the root. I knew they didn't mean for her to hear them, but I didn't care about the semantics. I didn't like their husbands, but they didn't see me walking up in their houses on some nonsense. A man was supposed to elevate the life of his woman. In my eyes, their husbands had failed. Instead, they downgraded them from the life they lived when they were single and my dad took care of them. But as long as they didn't put their hands on them, I'd mind my business.

Getting out of my reverie, I peered over the railing and Reign's eyes caught mine. I winked at her, and she gave me that smile I was fortunate to be the recipient of. We moved our relationship forward last night. Me telling her that she was mine. Even though we were pretending to be engaged, we'd developed real feelings for each other and wanted to explore where that would lead.

After I retired to my bedroom, sleep eluded me. Thoughts of Finley and how open I'd been for her haunted me. We met in my senior year of college, and I fell hard. She followed me to Phoenix when I got drafted and we moved in together. The adjustment period when I first got to the league was made easier with the knowledge that I got to come home to Finley. Like any relationship, we had our rocky times, but she was my ace. Or so I thought.

I guess being a baller's girl was more important than loyalty. After my accident, everyone in the media ran with the story that I might not play again. Apparently, she did too since she found her next baller in my then best friend, Vance Henderson.

I told myself I could trust Reign. I did trust her, but still I wondered. My pastor said not every thought needs to be fueled, so I tried not to dwell on it. This thing with Reign felt different.

I'd matured and she was a grown woman. My baby had her own money and was making moves for herself long before I came into play. I teased her often, reminding her of how she ran from me. Now, I noticed she always had to have some part of her on me if we were in close proximity. I wasn't mad at it—dang, I felt the same way.

On top of that, I was possessive of her time. That reminded me, I needed to go break up this chit chat she was having with my parents. We had moves to make before our flight later. I made my way inside my bedroom, about to step into the bathroom for a shower when there was a knock on my door.

"Come in."

"*Oga* Cheta, *oga* Jidenna is downstairs," the head of my domestic staff said.

My brows dipped. "Thank you, Agnes. Tell him to come up." I wondered since when he had to announce himself.

"*Oga*, I told him you were here, but he told me to tell you to come down."

"Okay, tell him to give me a minute."

Agnes left the way she came. She was a middle-aged woman and the longest member of staff I had. She had proven herself to me over the years and I took care of her over and beyond her salary. I knew that when I told her to watch out for Reign, she'd tell me if anything went wrong. What I didn't expect was to find her teaching Reign how to make some local dishes. At first, I was scared to taste the *nkwobi* and *nsala* they made. Reign's frown had me being brave, but I warned her that if I ended up not being able to make training camp, I was telling all of Atlanta she was to blame.

"Ah, ah, Nna, *ke kwanu?*" I greeted Jidenna, calling him by his nickname. "Why didn't you come upstairs?"

"You have a woman now, knucklehead. I can't roam around your house—"

"Huh?"

He cut his eyes and shook his head at me. "You're older; you supposed to get it."

Taking in what he said, I nodded and sat opposite him in the living room. Unlike Arinze, who carried himself like the no nonsense, older cousin he was, sue me, but I was in trouble a lot. So, over the years, Jidenna had perfected acting like he was King Solomon with endless wisdom. Especially where I was concerned. I didn't pay him any attention, being that he was as bad as I was. The difference was, he moved in silence.

"Weren't you supposed to be headed to Port Harcourt?" I asked.

He scratched his head. "I was *o*, but Uju had a whole episode, and I didn't want to leave her like that. I'm gonna take her with me, but I had to make sure I have someone that can travel with us."

I chuckled at my niece. She was spoiled and had her dad, in fact all of us, wrapped around her little finger. My cousin looked stressed. If I didn't have plans for Reign, I would've kept Uju so he could handle his business kid free. Once I told him this, he bowed his head in defeat.

"I hate to see my baby upset, but I'm beginning to think my mom and mama are right. Am I doing her a disservice trying to raise her by myself? With my schedule?"

I moved closer to him. "I wish Nze was here so we could collectively kick your behind. Don't even think of leaving my niece here in Enugu for them to raise."

He looked up at me. "My mom can't move to Atlanta, and I can't move with Uju to Nigeria, not now. The timing is all wrong and I have contract obligations I need to fulfill."

"Cuz, I know you don't wanna hear this and we haven't brought it up in a while, but you can start to date again, get married—"

He narrowed his eyes at me. "*E bia la.* I see the changes in you and I'm happy for you. But I keep telling you and Nze, I'm not doing that again."

I stood, wanting to say something. Remind him that I'd said the same thing after Finley. But it wasn't the same. This man's wife died. I was about to change the subject when Reign walked in. She waved at Jidenna and turned to me. They'd probably seen each other outside before he came in. The sparkle in her eyes, I was sure matched mine as she made her way toward me. I leaned down to kiss her lips.

"Rei, I ain't think I'd see the day when a woman will make my cousin a big softie," Jidenna laughed.

Reign blushed and buried her head in my chest.

I draped my arm around her neck. "I'd be that for my baby. But I'll still check a disrespectful fool in a minute."

"I thought she'd calmed all that down." Jidenna said.

I knew he was instigating because we had talked. He knew I was feeling Reign heavy. He was also there when I had to put a fool down. We were at a highlife lounge in town and Ifunanya and Reign had gone to the restroom. This guy in the booth next to us was openly lusting after her. Talking all loud like I wasn't sitting right there. When I visited home, there was always someone who thought they could try me. I always told them to forget this American accent and the fact they see me on television. I was still Cheta Kalu, that went to Providence High, before relocating to the United States. I never backed down from a fight when I knew a lesson had to be taught.

Reign raised her head. "Please don't get him started. I've told him that his arrogance is what has people trying to cut him down to size."

"Like my man Deion said, I can't help that my confidence offends their insecurities."

She raised herself on the tips of her toes and brushed her lips against mine. "True, but tone it down a bit."

"You love my confidence; you call it arrogance."

"Of course, I do. It's sexy. But balance is key, baby."

"School him, Reign." Jidenna said, getting up to leave.

I ignored them. "Where are the parentals? Hope they didn't give you any trouble."

Reign rolled her eyes at me. "Your grandma came by a while ago and your mom left with her. Papa said he has to go to the office."

Jidenna's eyes met mine. I knew we were thinking the same thing. Reign had been calling my dad, "Papa," but still referred to my mother as "your mom."

"I'm about to head out. Y'all be good," Jidenna said.

"Where's Uju?" Reign asked. "I haven't seen her today."

"She's being naughty and is supposed to be on punishment." He shook his head. "I bet my sister is doing the opposite of what I asked."

After asking Jidenna to take it easy on "her girl," Reign walked toward the kitchen while I saw Jidenna to the door. Minutes later, I walked up to Reign. Her head was in the refrigerator while Agnes stood to the side looking uncomfortable. I chuckled and told Agnes it was okay for her to leave. Reign closed the fridge with a bottle of malt in her hand. I walked up to her and lifted her to the top of the island while I went in search of the bottle opener.

"You not gonna keep scaring my staff." I opened the bottle for her. "Glass?"

She shook her head and took a sip straight from the bottle. "I didn't do anything. I already allow her to call me Madam. All I wanted to do was get my own drink."

I stood between her legs. "I told you—"

"I know what you said. You might be used to it, but it will take some time to get used to people waiting on me. I'm used to doing things myself."

"I like the sound of that." I kissed her neck.

Her brows dipped. "Sound of what?"

"You said 'getting used to'…"

"And?"

"Getting used to implies permanency. Is that what this is?"

She looked at her ring finger. "I already got this house on my finger, so I guess—"

"That ring ain't mine. That's my publicist's ring. When I put *my* ring on your finger, you'll know."

"You always have a smooth response."

"I'm Nyce, remember?"

"How can I forget?" She threaded her fingers through my beard.

A couple of beats passed by with our gazes locked on each other. I told her so much that it was almost cliché, but Reign was so beautiful to me. The glow of her skin, those deep brown eyes, high cheekbones and perky full lips had me caught in a trance I was reluctant to leave. This is what drew me to her from afar.

Now that I had gotten to know her, she was so much more than what attracted me to her. Now I desired her for so much more. Her heart, her mind, her values. She was far from perfect. She was grouchy, sometimes a pessimist, and stubborn. But my issues were more than hers, so who was I to complain?

"Go pack a bag," I said, taking us out of the space that would have me doing something I knew neither of us were ready for yet.

Being with Reign and not having her in my bed had to be one of the greatest tests of my self-control. I wasn't a crazed teenager who couldn't control his hormones, but what could I say, I loved to have sex. With Reign, that wasn't what I wanted to do. I wanted to do things right. I needed to do things right. When I had her in my bed, I wanted to make love to her. Remove all doubt that she belonged to me. With how we came together and the stuff between us, I knew now wasn't the right time to go there with her.

"Why? I thought we were going to Rwanda after the chief-taincy ceremony. And aren't Jas and Arinze supposed to be—"

"*Asa*," I called out, halting her rundown. "Nze and Jas don't arrive until Monday. But we're not leaving the country. I wanna take you somewhere. You trust me?"

"Of course," she said, not missing a beat.

"All right then." I helped her down and grabbed her hand, heading out of the kitchen.

I watched, half annoyed and half amused at Reign as she strolled around the billiards table. The eight ball was left, and it was her turn. Instead of playing, she was dancing around gloating at her imminent victory. My competitive nature wouldn't allow me to take this beatdown without an attitude. Despite the mug I knew I had on my face, I loved how carefree she was.

When I met Reign, eighty percent of the time, she was dressed in some matching professional looking set, she wore her locs in a low bun and heels adorned her feet. I wouldn't call her uptight, but she was always so serious. Like she had to be on the straight and narrow all the time. I smiled, looking at her now, in her capri jeans, a multi-colored tank top and orange sandals on her well-manicured feet. The white polish had me suspecting I was a feet man and that had never been the case.

"Are you going to shoot or we gonna be dancing out here all night?"

"Aww baby, are *you dey vexed?*"

I wanted to be mad, but laughed instead at how she butchered the Pidgin English phrase. Since I wasn't going to let my baby be clowned on my watch, correcting her became paramount.

"It's *you dey vex?* Not are you dey vexed." I kissed her forehead.

"Okay, how do I say I'm about to whoop your behind?" She giggled and hunched over the table.

Reign positioned her cue stick and hit the cue ball. The ball sailed across the table to the eight ball, which sunk into the corner pocket. Reign began to do the running man before she broke into her own made-up version of the *azonto*, a Ghanian dance.

"It's two of the three. I won one, you won this one. Cheating of course." I leaned against the table.

"How did I cheat?"

"You knew what you were doing when you took off your shirt, leaving this tank top." I knew she did it on purpose because after discarding her shirt, she kept batting her eyes and wiggling in front of me.

Reign laughed. "I'm not—"

"Don't tell me you won?" Arinze's cousin, Qasif, asked, entering our private area.

The waiter with our food and drinks trailed behind him. Reign exaggerated her win to him while I pointed the waiter to who ordered what and where to place it. Last night when we arrived Ibadan, I called Qasif to let him know we'd arrived and asked the time for the tour. During that conversation and in typical Adeshina style, his parents insisted we stayed on their estate. There was no sense arguing with them, so I acquiesced. We were accommodated in one of their guest houses.

Once we were settled, I took Reign out to eat in one of the most romantic spots in the town. We had a great meal and danced some of the calories off afterwards. The reaction on her face and the gratitude in her eyes was totally worth the silent treatment she gave me when I refused to tell her where we were going.

Early this morning, Qasif arrived to take us on the tour of the farm. I knew they had people who did this, and I wasn't looking for any special treatment since I knew everyone was busy. So, I didn't expect Qasif to personally handle the tour, but he did. Like my cousins and I, he and his brothers knew every part of the family business.

Reign sat in awe and was so full of questions when we toured the 75,000-acre farm. Then we went to visit the site where shea butter was made. I stayed a safe distance behind while Reign asked the lead cosmetologist all the questions she desired. At a point, she took out her phone and began taking notes. A few hours later, Qasif took us to out for lunch before he left to handle business and we'd chilled by the pool in the estate.

It was now the next afternoon and I'd remembered this place called Koko Dome and decided it would be the perfect relaxation spot. The atmosphere was chill, with old school Afrobeats being the theme for the night. Qasif arrived to meet us here right before Reign started her round. I made a mental note to tell Arinze to thank his cousins for me. I'm pretty sure playing host wasn't in his plans for the weekend, but he seemed to turn his whole schedule around to accommodate us.

"We're about to go again once we eat." I pulled Reign down on my lap.

"No, we're not. I'm tired." She picked up her zobo and took a sip. "Besides, I might beat him again and then it'll be a whole thing."

Qasif laughed. "I know right? We can't have him in his feelings."

"I'm glad you think this is funny. I'mma about to leave you here. This guy can bring you back home," I teased.

She kissed my cheek before turning her focus to Qasif. "I wanted to tell you earlier, but you stepped away. Your farm is huge, and the operation runs seamlessly. In my mind, when I think of farming, something a little bigger than my mother's garden comes to mind. I mean, I know a farm can be so much more, but being on one...impressive."

"Thank you. It's a family effort that started with my grandfather, then my father. My brothers and I have tried to bring it to the 21st century," Qasif said.

Their conversation shifted to the history of Ibadan. When most people thought of Nigeria, Lagos, Abuja or Port Harcourt came to mind. However, there were other cities that had so much to offer. Ibadan, which was a two-hour drive away from Lagos, was one of them. My phone buzzed and I removed it to see a text.

Nze: I'm in Boston and you won't believe who I just saw

My forehead creased. **What are you doing in Boston?**

He was supposed to be in Atlanta getting ready to head to Nigeria. He better not be about to tell me he wasn't going to make it.

Nze: Chill out. I'll be there.

I smiled because he knew me so well. I sent him a high five emoji.

Nze: I was ordering something for Jas when Finley walked up to me.

I frowned. **What did she want?**

Nze: She told me to tell you guard drop. What does that mean?

I stilled.

Reign must've noticed it too because she turned toward me. "You, okay?"

"Yeah, I'm cool. It's Nze." My eyes darted to Qasif, and he gave me a slight nod.

We weren't that cool, but as a guy, I'm sure he read my body language. The nod was to tell me that he'd keep Reign occupied.

It's nothing. Hope you told her to keep it moving.

I know u lying but I'll see you Monday.

Bet.

I pocketed my phone as Reign brought a piece of suya up to my lips. Taking the piece of meat into my mouth, I rejoined the conversation. At the back of my mind though, I needed to send a clear message back to Finley. Arinze was right. I was lying.

Guard drop, as in stripping down our guard or walls, used to be our code when we needed to be completely vulnerable with each other. Once we said it, whatever was said between us couldn't be used as a weapon in an argument. Unlike Arinze who ignored his ex, forcing her to pop up on him during his movie premiere, when we broke up, I had told Finley everything I wanted to say. I was happy. For the first time since we split, I was genuinely happy.

My free hand caressed Reign's back. Not that it was anything to be proud of, but I'd been with numerous women since our breakup. Not once had Finley deemed it fit to reach out. Reign being my fiancée had to be the trigger. That was her problem because nothing she had to say was of interest to me. Before she interpreted my silence for something it wasn't, I was going to have to reach out to her and make it clear again. Nothing was messing up what I had going on.

10

REIGN

The low breeze and the air coming from the huge fans made the heat somewhat manageable. I trained my mind on the positive because if I thought about how I was really feeling, my expression would mirror it. I dared not appear in a video with a stank face. God forbid a photographer captured a shot with the deep crease in my forehead.

I fanned myself with the program as I listened to who was introduced as the chairman of the council of chiefs give a speech. We were in the football field of one of the primary schools in town. The canopies, which were placed in an L shape around the area, were occupied by the who's who of Enugu and its surrounding areas to honor Cheta's dad on the conferment of his chieftaincy title. The sole reason for being in Nigeria was finally here and it wasn't anything like Cheta explained. His description paled in comparison to the fanfare I was currently witnessing. He kept reassuring me it was no big deal. Oh, how he was wrong.

By the time we got back from Ibadan a few days ago, preparations were in full swing. The Kalu estate was buzzing with activity. Groundskeepers, event planners, caterers, live bands, DJ's, you name it, were in and out of the compound. All in preparation for the reception that would be happening after this.

I refocused my attention to the podium, specifically admiring my man. Cheta stood next to his father, looking as regal as a king. He wore a cream, short-sleeved tunic shirt, sort of like a dashiki, but it was made of some high-quality suede material. The material had the head of a lion printed on it. The shirt, which I was told was called the *Isiagu,* was worn over black pants. He traded in his Cuban link for a long, red bead chain he wore around his neck which matched the two pieces on his wrist. On his head was a black cap. He looked amazing. His cousins wore the same thing, but their shirts were black instead of cream. I turned to my left where Jasmine and Arinze sat, engrossed in each other. All members of the Kalu family were seated in the canopy I was in. I turned to my back where Jidenna was. I touched his leg to get his attention.

"After this speech, what happens?" I whispered.

Leaning closer to me, he said. "They will confer my uncle with the title, then he will give his speech. Give and take about an hour and a half, it will be all over. Then the party moves to the estate."

I nodded. "And Papa being a chief doesn't mean he has subjects. It's almost like an honorary degree kinda thing, right?"

Jidenna smiled, something he rarely did. "In a way, yes. He won't rule over anybody."

I turned back around to concentrate on what was being said. It was as though Cheta sensed my gaze because I felt his eyes on me through the sunshades he wore. I had been so wrong about him. He was everything I didn't even know I needed. He was still everything that made him Nyce, but the side he'd been showing me had me falling for him fast. I knew my feelings for him were becoming deeper, right from when we went to the mountains for that weekend. But our trip to Ibadan showed me that he was more than a smooth charmer. He listened to and cared about my dreams. The surprise trip to the farm and the shea butter plant brought tears to my eyes.

"God created man in His image. In doing so, He instructed us to do good works on earth. Mr. Chima Kalu has expressed God's likeness in him by working hard to make our community better through development initiatives. We thank God that made him a source of His blessings on our community."

The ruler continued by listing the impressive projects Cheta's father had worked on and contributed to the community outside of the joint family charities. Several minutes later, he was done. After a round of applause, Cheta helped his dad kneel on a cushioned stoop before the ruler, then he stood behind him. His uncles, Jidenna and Arinze's dads, stood to either side of him. The ruler placed his hand on Cheta's father's head and spoke in Igbo, the native language.

A few minutes later, an aide handed the ruler a red cap that had a long white feather in it and he placed it on Cheta's father's head. He said a few more words of something I assumed was prayer then Cheta's dad stood up. A man with a flute-like instrument started to blow and dancers came out.

I was so engrossed in what was happening that I didn't notice Cheta's mom appear before me. She extended her hand, and I placed mine in it. I was totally confused on where we were going. However, that was quickly cleared up as we started dancing toward the men. Well, she danced. I swayed from left to right as much as I could. I looked behind me and Jasmine was right there. I was about to say something to her when I saw Cheta strolling toward me.

"You good?" He kissed my cheek.

I raised my hand to lift his sunshades slightly so I could see his face. "I'm fine, but worried about you."

"Why?"

"You still haven't eaten anything."

"*Asa m*, I'm good. Stop worrying. We'll soon leave for the house."

I frowned, but he pulled me into him and tried to teach me some steps. I had barely seen him all day. The minute we woke up this morning, he was out of the house. He had told me how being a son came with responsibilities. His cousins helped, but he was still the only son of his parents. He'd been with his dad, making sure everything went off without a hitch. A few hours after he left, Ifunanya arrived, and she and I went to Arinze's house where Jasmine was waiting for us to get dressed.

Many hours later that night, Jidenna rubbed his hands together. His eyes darted between Jasmine and her man, and me and mine. "Last two questions. Nze, you and Jas are ahead by four points. But Rei and Cheta have been on a streak, so what's it gonna be?"

It had been a long, tiring day, but surprisingly we were still wired, and what started off as us watching a movie in Cheta's movie room, turned into game night. Smooth R&B floated in the background of the dimly lit room, providing the perfect ambience to a chill night compared to an otherwise busy day. My eyes darted to the wall clock. It was a few minutes before midnight.

The activity of earlier had died down and older Kalus had called it a night. When we arrived back at the estate earlier after the ceremony, the huge area in the middle of the estate resembled a carnival. Food, music, traditional dancers, an all-round celebration. The party lasted way into the evening before guests began to leave.

Arinze kissed Jasmine on her cheek and asked if she wanted to continue. She answered yes. I was glad she did, since I was the reason we were down four points. We were playing *This or That* and I wanted to redeem myself. The competitive spirit in me had taken over. That coupled with Cheta being so extra with his overdramatic display of hurt over the fact that I didn't know him.

We weren't playing by the traditional rules. Instead, we had to guess the answers our partners would give. Jidenna was the moderator and scorekeeper. Arinze and Jasmine were so in sync and it was a beautiful thing to watch. Surprisingly, Cheta knew a lot more about me than I thought he did.

"It's okay if you tired, baby." Cheta let out an exaggerated sigh.

I rolled my eyes.

"I mean, it's cool if I die because you wanna give me a strawberry cake." He shrugged.

The others laughed and I shook my head. "Will you stop saying that?" How was I supposed to know he was allergic to strawberries?

"I mean, I can see the Netflix movie now. Untold. Cheta Kalu, three-time MVP, poisoned by fiancée." He demonstrated with his hands at some imaginary billboard.

"Whatever." I sucked my teeth.

He chuckled, nuzzling his nose in the crook of my neck. "Come on, baby, as long as you're the one that kills me, I'm good."

I shrugged him off. "Cheta, get off me."

I was becoming more irritated with all the laughter. I knew he was joking, but the idea of him dying didn't sit well with me and I didn't want him joking about it. I tried to stand up from my seat on his lap, but he held me tighter.

"Okay, my bad, my bad. But for real, we got a flight to catch in the morning. You sure you don't wanna call it?"

"I'm good."

Jidenna clapped his hands. "Next question. Jas, for Nze, planned or spontaneous getaways?"

Arinze and Jasmine exchanged knowing glances.

Jasmine pointed to herself. "I'd rather get up and go, but Mr. Hollywood over here has to be planned out in advance."

Arinze laughed. "I see you got jokes. But your joke is about to put us behind because although I have to plan, I prefer spontaneous."

"Same difference," Jasmine shrugged.

"Nah, Jazzy Jas. Y'all gotta take the L." Cheta tilted his head to the side.

I danced on his lap. "Come on, Jide, we got next."

Cheta squeezed my waist and I turned to look at him. He blew me a kiss.

"Rei, would your man rather have three hands or three legs?"

"Rei, you bet not mess this up," Cheta threatened.

Jasmine giggled and covered her eyes.

Arinze waved his hands in the air and shook his head. "Nna, ask something else because if your cousin says the wrong thing in front of my wife, I'm going to beat him."

"Okay, y'all chill out. Three hands for making all those nets. Right, babe?"

"You got it. Go ahead and mark it. We won." Cheta pulled me closer and whispered. "Good answer. You know I got three legs already?"

My mouth dropped and I elbowed him. "You know what..."

Although I was sure nobody else heard what he said, they knew it was crass. They laughed, well everybody except Arinze. If I didn't know better, I'd think he was always so serious. Cheta tapped my thigh and I moved to the seat next to him. He stood and turned on the light.

"It's all love, but y'all need to head out," Cheta said.

I sighed. "Rude as can be. Sorry guys—"

"We're supposed to be on the same team, Rei. Why you making me look bad? They know I love them, but—"

"You're special. Yeah, we know." Jasmine said.

Arinze pulled her up. We wouldn't be able to hang out again until we got to Atlanta. Cheta and I were heading to Rwanda in the morning, while they all were headed to America the day after. After I said my goodbyes, Cheta walked them out while I shot Ebonie a quick text with an update on my arrival. What was supposed to be two weeks away was turning into two weeks and some days. While I thoroughly enjoyed my stay in Nigeria, I missed my regular routine. I had a lot of stuff to get done with the new direction I was headed in with Coleman and I couldn't wait to get started.

Cheta squeezed my hand as we trailed behind Peter, our tour guide. I could feel my steps falter as we walked further into the Kigali Genocide Memorial. At first, I didn't want to do this tour, but then I wouldn't forgive myself if I came all this way and didn't take the opportunity to learn about the devastation of 1994 that hit this country. I remembered our pastor in church talking about it when it was time to make donations for some cause. I went home that day and researched it.

My first thought was that the entire world sat back and did nothing while people were dying. Almost a million people died because of ethnic differences. If this country had been in Europe or Northern America, it would have gotten way more attention than it did. Way more attention than a Hollywood movie made after the fact.

We were in the last hour of the two-hour tour and all I could say was that it was a profoundly moving experience that would stay with me forever. I was happy I decided to do this instead of the safari, canopy walk, or lake tours Cheta had suggested. The narrative and accompanying imagery held nothing back, so I did shed a few tears, but the story of reconciliation and forgiveness was also powerful. If there was ever a country that could be named the comeback kid, it was Rwanda.

This was the last day of our three-day stay in the country also called the land of a thousand hills. The first day, we were beat, so stayed in our suite at the Marriott, sleeping and eating the day away. The day after, Cheta had to do the stuff he came here to do with the Basketball Africa League. The league had chosen the current top basketballers from the North, West, East and

Southern parts of Africa as ambassadors to do promotional rounds. This was the only time all four players were free, so the league crammed as much as they could in one day.

Being late September, training camp was about to start, so Cheta and one other guy that played in the NBA had to get back to the US. We spent the day being chauffeured from one television or radio station to the other. Then there was a photo shoot in the Kigali Stadium and some other areas around town. It was then I got to see how clean this city was. It was so far away from the tragedy that befell it all those years ago.

There was a full day when people couldn't drive their cars, a measure aimed at reducing pollution, promoting exercise and healthy living. It was also interesting to me that the country's original name was Ruanda-Urundi. But the Belgians urged the UN to divide it into two countries, Rwanda, and today's Burundi. The audacity of these Europeans.

"We are now at the end of the tour where five mass graves are. Here lies the remains of thousands of people. Please be respectful of the area as family members of the deceased might be among you, or are there were they often come to reflect," the guide announced.

I pulled on Cheta's hand, and he leaned in. "Have you been to the 9/11 memorial in New York?"

He nodded.

"It's the same thing they tell you there too. Not to lean on the names and stuff."

"I know, but I feel people should know that regardless."

"True."

"You hungry?"

"Yeah, but I don't know if I'd have an appetite after this." I pulled him toward the exit because my peripheral caught two guys with an excited look on their face coming towards us.

That was the look I had become used to when his fans approached. I'd insisted on us doing the tour with others instead of a private tour. I quickly regretted that when a few people asked for a selfie and autograph before we started. Who does that? In this place of all places.

"It's sad history, but exists so we can learn from it. That has nothing to do with your stomach. Besides, you wanted to come here. We could have been chilling by the lake or be chugging some milk."

"Eww…not to knock it, but no thank you. Now let's finish here so we can eat."

"Your wish is my command."

I shuddered when I remembered our trip to what was called a milk bar. We were told that they only existed in Kigali. Nowhere else in all of East Africa had them. They were actual pubs that sold nothing but milk. Cold, hot, fermented, fresh, big, medium, small, to go, drink in, refills, they had it all in these milk bars. They were like bars but instead of beer, they sold milk. It had something to do with the country's history, culture and relationship with cows. But chugging milk was not my idea of a good time. I could say that I tried it though.

Several hours later, Cheta and I sat on the balcony of our suite. My legs were on his lap as he massaged my feet. The rest of the tour took us to the parliament which was equivalent to the Capitol in the US. It was run by three quarters women. Next a local market and finally ending at the city plaza. My soul, stomach and mind were full. This trip owed me nothing. Now, we sat in comfortable silence taking in the fresh air and stunning scenery of the hills in the distance.

"What do you think?" Cheta's voice brought me out of my head.

"About?"

"This, the trip. How was it? Was it what you expected?"

I took in a breath. "Quite frankly, I didn't know what to expect. With the internet, I did know that Africa wasn't like what we were shown on TV growing up. But I was pleasantly surprised. I learned a whole lot. Enugu being the coal city, Ibadan, and its rich history, here...I mean. If we keeping it a buck, I was more apprehensive about your family."

Cheta nodded. "And now?"

I shrugged. "Your sisters and I have an understanding, Ify is my girl. Your grandpa, pops and uncles are so sweet." I laughed to myself. "I think your grandma and mother are neutral, or they have an opinion, but kept it to themselves."

Cheta pinned me with his gaze. He'd been a pensive since we got back to the hotel earlier. I wasn't used to this solemn part of him. I'd asked what was bothering him a few times, but he always replied it was nothing.

"Come here."

I stood and closed the distance between us. He pulled me down to his lap. I repositioned myself so my legs crossed over his. Sitting sideways, I could see his face. We sat for a moment in silence while he rubbed my back in a circular motion.

"What's wrong?" I asked.

He stared at me for a beat. "I wanna tell you something, but I got something to ask you first."

Nervousness rumbled in my belly. "Okay..."

"Your phone has been buzzing a lot today. Since I've known you, that has never been the case. Which tells me it's someone you either don't want me to know about, or you don't wanna talk to them. I'm not feeling either scenario—"

"It's not—"

"Don't play me, Reign. I'm not proud to admit it, but I know those games. I've played them, but I've always been truthful with you."

"And I have been with you. What I was going to say was, it's not something I wanted to deal with now."

"Who is it?"

"Martrell. He—"

"Ex-boyfriend that wanted you barefoot and pregnant overseas, Martrell?"

I snickered, not because it was funny, well his description was, but the look on his face was pure evil.

"I don't know what's so funny."

"You are funny. Yes, him. He says he wants to talk—"

"About what? Rei, don't be like Jas and end up with your feelings hurt. I ain't that mature yet. You hurt me and I get even."

I stood because he was about to make me slap him. Jasmine had told me that she and Arinze had a period of separation because she thought it was wise to meet up with her ex, but lied to Arinze about it. I narrowed my eyes at him, and he leaned back in his chair like he wasn't bothered.

"Get even then…good night." Done with this silly discussion, I brushed past him and opened the sliding door. I hadn't gotten into the suite good when I felt Cheta pull me back. I struggled against him, but his hold was tight. His lips were on my neck. He peppered light kisses as he repeated his apology.

"My bad. Sorry babe."

I kissed him back, accepting his apology.

He looked at me, his expression concerned. "So, what does he want to talk about?"

"Look, I know why you don't trust easy, but I'll never intentionally hurt you." I sighed. I was about to reveal something I'd known for weeks. In the moment he insinuated me being with someone else, I knew for sure it was real. "I love you. He—"

"Nah, you can't tell me you love me then try to talk about another man. Say it again."

I yelped as Cheta lifted me. My legs went around his waist as he walked to the bar area. He sat me on the bar. I cupped his face. In between kisses on his lips, I repeated myself. "I love you."

"I love you too. That's what I wanted to tell you. So much that it legit got me scared. I haven't let myself get close to anyone in over five years. Then here you go, less than a year and I can't see my life without you. When we get back, we're gonna be so busy. In case you haven't noticed, I'm possessive, clingy and a little crazy. But I'll never do anything that will hinder your shine or have you looking stupid. Promise me you'll do the same."

"Yeah, I've noticed, but I love you for it." We shared a laugh. "I promise. I know we'll be busy, but if we prioritize us, we'll be fine." A beat passed between us. "Now, can I tell you what Martrell wants?"

"Yeah, go ahead."

"We bought a property a while ago and now that I'm someone else's headache...his words not mine...he wants to sell it so I can...throw away my life with a bad boy...again his words not mine."

Cheta's expression dulled and he let out a dry laugh. It wasn't the sound that had humor in it, but evil. "Hmm...tell him to send you the papers. You don't need to see him. *Asa*, don't have me losing my home training."

"You gonna stop threatening me with your little tantrums."

"It ain't a threat, baby. Now kiss me."

Cheta gripped the back on my neck, crashing our lips together, passionately causing my body to hum and my heart to stutter. This man had me so far gone that the thought of returning had me terrified.

11

CHETA

I adjusted my bowtie and tapped on Reign's front door for the second time. I told this woman I was on my way, and I could bet anything she still wasn't ready. Blowing out a cool breath from the chilly April evening, I glanced at my watch. We were still doing good on time, but I didn't want to cut it too close. I wanted to walk the red carpet with my cousins. Being with them would hopefully spread the spotlight around.

I lifted my hand again when the door flew open. I was ready to go in on her, but all that was paused when I took her in. My eyes shamelessly roamed her petite frame clad in a dark green, sequined dress. Her hair was up in a bun, exposing the neck I loved biting on. On her feet were some Louboutin heels that brought her up to my upper chest. The only jewelry she wore were the diamond droplets I had gotten her for Christmas.

"Are you going to come in or keep staring at me from the door?"

I stepped into her condo and used the back of my foot to slam the door shut. Her eyes sparkled and I pulled her close to me, wrapping both arms around her.

"You got any more of that?" I pointed to her lips.

"What? My lipstick? Yeah—"

"Good, cos I'm about to take this off." I cupped her face and kissed her deeply.

"Oh wow. What was that for?"

"Can't I kiss my woman? You act like you don't miss me. I've been away for three weeks."

"Oh, don't be a baby. I've flown to be with you one of those weeks."

"Okay, I see how it is. Forget you then." I feigned trying to remove her arms from around my waist.

She laughed at me and held on tighter. "I'm sorry. I love you. But you know I hate it when you're gone." She puckered her lips and I gave her what she wanted.

"Better act like it." I kissed her forehead. "I love you too."

"I've told you about your silly threats." Her eyes roamed my body. "You always clean up nice." She admired the black, three-piece, single-breasted, evening tuxedo I had on.

"Thanks, my love. You look beautiful as well." I placed my hand on her lower back as we walked further into her home. The citrusy vanilla aroma wafted lightly through the house, cementing its homey feel.

"How was San Antonio?" She headed toward the stairs.

I grabbed her hand. "Baby, come on. Where are you going? We're going to be late."

She patted my chest. "Bae, relax, I'll be right down. I promise."

Reluctantly, I let her go. I was not trying to argue with her tonight. In the last six months, we'd had the time of our lives and the arguments to match. Nothing so major that we ever considered parting ways, but Reign and I were pretty much the same when it came to our opinions. We rarely backed down.

Sometimes things got heated, but we also had set boundaries. A major one being never to walk out or hang up on the other. There would be times we'd be mad at each other and still sit and watch a movie together. If she needed space, there was a particular room in my house that was her "space" room. I didn't care as far as she didn't leave when we were on the outs.

My cousins and I were attending a charity event for our alma mater. Morehouse College shaped us, so any time we were invited for something and could attend, we did. Also tonight, Jidenna was bringing Zola. She was Uju's dance teacher. He swore it was only because he didn't want to walk in solo. Arinze and I thought it was more than that. But whatever the reason, we were glad he was bringing anyone at all.

I unbuttoned my tux and sat down on the couch. I felt a paper under me, so I lifted a little and pulled it out. Browsing over it, I saw it was about the rental property Reign had with ol' boy. Also with it was a letter asking for confirmation of her arrival to Savannah to do a walk-through.

My brows furrowed as heat rose within me. I thought this matter was handled. As a matter of fact, I specifically remembered her telling me she signed the papers. Nah, there had to be some explanation why she gave dude the idea she was meeting up with him. I didn't trust him, and neither should she.

"I'm ready," she sang from behind me.

I closed my eyes, took in a breath, praying for God to help me say the right thing. I stood with the papers in my hand. "What's this?"

Reign stared at me like a deer caught in headlights. She didn't look at my hand because she knew what I was holding.

"I was going to talk to you about that."

"When? And you still haven't answered my question."

"Look, I know what you said—"

"I said? We agreed!" I roared. I hadn't wanted to raise my voice, but the way she was trying to handle me was sending me over.

"Don't raise your voice at me." She placed her hand on her hips. "You said, we agreed, whatever. The first deal fell through because it didn't appraise for how much it was supposed to be worth. Martrell did some upgrades and now we both have to be—"

"That's crap. You don't have to be anywhere."

"I'm not Finley!"

"What did you just say to me? Really? That's what we do now?" I intertwined my fingers and steepled my indexes under my lower lip. "I don't trust him. He's been doing everything to get you to Savannah. When I'm free to go with you, he suddenly can't make it. But you know what? You got it. Do what you wanna do. I'm not saying another word."

I couldn't believe she brought up Finley. I bared my soul to her. Everything about that relationship. Told her when Finley tried to contact me through Arinze. I even had her with me when I called Finley and made my stand clear, after which I blocked her number. That's the thing with women, they say we're closed off. But when you talk, they wanna use that very thing against you.

"Babe, I'm sorry. I want you to trust me. I—"

"And I do. This isn't about trust. This is about not putting yourself in situations that can backfire. But I'm done talking." I walked around her to the door. I could feel her watching me and although I loved her, I had nothing else for her. I opened the door and waited for her to stroll toward me. When she got to me, she stopped. I met her eyes, but my expression was aplomb.

"Can we talk about this later?"

"Nah, ain't nothing to talk about."

She walked out and I took her keys from her to lock the door. I'd been talking about this since she first brought it up. It was always one thing after the other with the guy. But since she wanted to do it her way, I'd let her. She better hope and pray that I was wrong.

With my hand on the small of her back, I walked her to my Mercedes-AMG G55. Once she was buckled in, I walked around to let myself in. I started the car and pulled out of her driveway.

Glancing over at Reign, I could feel her unease. Grabbing her hand, I intertwined our fingers. Her touch calmed me and helped me get my mind right. I needed that to at least look like I was happy.

~

With both hands stuffed in my pockets, my eyes scanned the room filled with celebrities and regular people all successful in their own right. My vision landed and settled on the woman who had my head all messed up. In a good way, but still messed up. The networking part of the event was underway and Reign was currently standing with Mrs. Safiya Gray. She and her billionaire husband, Darius Gray were well known Atlanta personalities.

My heart swelled with a familiar feeling of satisfaction. I was so proud of my woman. Her business was doing mad numbers. She'd officially opened her new warehouse to accommodate the business from Coleman Hospitality. She'd hired a few more staff and was balancing her business and our relationship like a pro. Although she kicked against it, I hosted a huge celebration dinner for her opening. Surprisingly, her parents honored my invitation for the dinner. So, along with my family, a few of my closest boys and their significant others, we celebrated my girl.

My game has been top notch since the season started. In addition to winning and the points I put down each night, the highlight of most of my games was knowing she was courtside cheering me on. Life was great and I could confidently say that this was the happiest I'd been in a very long time. My family was good, no complaints there, but my relationship was even better.

Over the past couple of months, the blogs continued to hound us. They went from reposting my past dirt, to doubting our engagement, then slowly moving on to "couple goaling" our every move. The woman I loved and who also rattled me like no one else remained solid, no matter what headline we were on any day.

This week, I'd be leaving for the first game of the East Conference finals, and I didn't want to be distracted by worrying about her. I didn't trust that Martrell dude and nothing Arinze or Jidenna could say could make me believe otherwise.

"Cuzzo, you see the way you are looking at her now." I turned to listen to Arinze. "You're going to ruin what y'all got going on if you continue acting like she can't take care of herself."

Nze, Jidenna, and I were huddled up in the corner, nursing our drinks with our eyes trained on our women. Well… Jasmine and Reign. We weren't quite sure what Zola was. Jidenna was tight lipped, but they looked comfortable with each other.

I waved him off and took a sip of my drink. "I don't know why you guys don't hear what I'm saying."

"We hear you, but we don't agree. Leave Rei to handle her business. She isn't Finley." Jidenna shrugged.

"And if you keep fussing, she'll think you don't trust her. Ho—"

"How many times will I say it's not her I don't trust. It—"

"*Hapụ ihe ahụ* Don't sabotage this thing because of your insecurities."

I sniggered. "You of all people know that I'm not insecure. But like I told her, I'm done talking about it. I got some days before I head out of town. All I want to do is enjoy my woman in peace."

My cousins grunted. They knew me—once I shut down a topic that was it. We were going to have to agree to disagree. The only reason we were discussing it was that they'd sensed the uneasy energy between Reign and I when we walked in. After being around them for countless family outings, they'd come to recognize our overly emotional vibe, as they called it.

"Speaking of women—"

Jidenna shook his head. "We weren't speaking of women. We were speaking of your overprotective behind."

Arinze laughed because he knew exactly where I was headed. Jidenna was trying to throw me off. They were all in my business, so I was about to be in his.

"Yeah, whatever, speaking of women. What's up with Teach?" I asked.

Jidenna's brows furrowed. "Teach?"

"This guy...you love giving out nicknames," Arinze said.

My brows dipped at Arinze. "Ain't that what she is?" I turned to Jidenna. "So, about—"

"About nothing. I—"

"Ladies and gentlemen..."

The voice of the host interrupted his spiel. Jidenna raised his glass to me with a smirk as we listened to the host asking us to return to our seats for the next phase of the night. The women began walking towards us. Meeting her halfway, I pulled Reign close and kissed her lips briefly, before leading her back to our table. I couldn't wait for this to be over so we could chill out and enjoy each other's company.

I decided to do take my cousins' advice and stop tripping about her upcoming trip to Savannah. I knew she could handle herself. The sooner she did whatever needed to be done, the sooner we could have that man out of our lives.

I crept up behind Reign who was standing in front of her bathroom mirror, applying a facial mask. My arms circled her waist, causing her to jump.

Nuzzling her neck, I chuckled lightly. "You owe someone money?"

"No, move. You scared me." Craning her neck, she looked up at me. "You're going to get that stuff on me.

"I don't wanna hear it. You should've thought about that before forcing me to put it on."

She shook her head. "Something is wrong with you."

Lifting her, I placed her on the bathroom counter. "You are. You not done? I'm about to restart the movie."

She gave me that smile I lived for and raised her hand to smooth out the mask I had on. It had been a week since the charity event, and I had done exactly what I wanted to do which was enjoy my woman's company. We'd gotten enough of the media attention, so we decided to do low key stuff that could be done in my house or hers. Painting, mini golf at my backyard, crafting and couples cooking tutorials.

I had a flight to catch later tonight, so I'd been laid up at her place most of the day. After lunch, she chose *Love & Basketball* for us to watch. With my head in her lap, she explained why considering the movie a love story was one of the biggest scams in movie history. As her fingers grazed my face, she came up on a pimple by my temple. For the skincare queen, that was an abomination.

Subsequently I got a lecture on not using the products she'd packed for me as she instructed. She was right though. Some nights when I got back to my hotel room, all I wanted to do was take a shower, and check in with her before dozing off. Reign wasn't trying to hear that though, so she made me wear the mask I currently had on. Since I wasn't the only one about to be looking like a masquerade in the middle of the day, I got her to wear one with me.

A few pecks later, I helped Reign down and led her to the living room. On our way, she stopped by the kitchen to get her favorite flavor of ice cream, butter pecan, and two spoons. Even in the winter, my baby could eat ice cream all day. Now that she was on her cycle, it was a whole event.

The first time I saw her do it and joked about it, the lid came flying across the room, aimed at my forehead. Now, I let her do her while I "yes babe'd" or rubbed her back as she needed it. A few minutes later, Reign began her litany of complaints again. I had nothing to add, but if it was that bad, why watch it? Better yet, why torture me? I felt Reign's eyes on me. Taking a spoonful of ice cream, I mindlessly rubbed her foot, something that had become one of my favorite past times. "Why you staring at me?"

"I can't look at my man no more?" She licked her spoon and I chuckled at her using my words back at me.

"You got that. But I know you, so what's up?"

She set the ice cream carton on the coffee table, then let out a deep sigh. "Babe, I head to Savannah after work tomorrow."

I turned, hiking my brow. "Whatchu mean tomorrow?"

Reign removed her feet from my lap. Unlike before, I didn't stop her. She sat up and I rubbed my palms against my thighs to calm myself down. It was Wednesday evening, and Game One of the conference finals was in two days. We'd planned she'd fly to Boston for the game on Friday, and then turn around and fly back Saturday morning in time for a pop-up event she had in the city.

"Remember I was supposed to go Sunday, see the realtor on Monday, and be back that evening."

I remained silent because as I recalled, the Martrell guy was cool with her moving their meet to next week. Sunday afternoon, she'd found out that a batch of one of her products didn't come out right. I remember meeting her at her shop the next morning. While she worked on creating a new batch, I helped Ebonie pack orders. It was an all-hands-on deck kinda morning.

"Well, Martrell says he has to leave the country next week, so we have to get it done tomorrow." Before I could say anything, she quickly added. "I promise, right after, I'll be on a plane headed your way."

I stood. "Ain't nothing I'll say that you won't have an argument for, and I'm not about to do that with you." I leaned over her with both my hands on the back of the sofa, encasing her in.

"*Asa m*, don't be there though, and I'mma show my entire behind." I kissed her forehead and walked toward her bathroom.

It was time to take this stuff off my face and head home. I had a game to win.

Two days later, the sound of the net popped just as the buzzer went off. I was a bit off my game all night, but I had pulled my team through in the final quarter. I'd narrowly landed the final three-point shot, ending the game. We'd won with a single-digit lead. I would've liked for it to be double, but I'd take a win any way I could get it. Especially with the way I was currently feeling.

As the team rushed to the floor, dapping, and tugging me in different directions, my eyes continued to dart to the second row. That was where Reign should've been, but the text I received at half-time gave me some flimsy reason behind her absence. All the emotions I thought I'd worked on over the last few months suddenly surged to the surface. The shame, disgrace, and humiliation I had faced with Finley suddenly reared their ugly head. I had put in the work to let go of my trust issues, but her missing her flight because she was with another man didn't sit well with me. Especially considering who it was. I needed more than a "the meeting went over."

Zane walked towards me, and we slapped hands. "Good job, man. For a second, you had me shook."

"But God." I pointed to the ceiling as we headed to the back. Normally, whenever Reign attended my games, she'd be waiting for me at the corner of the tunnel. It wasn't the case today. Instead, Coach Reynolds stopped me.

"I need you and Zane to do the post-game interview."

"Nah, Coach, I can't do it tonight. I gotta—"

"If it's not a family emergency, I don't wanna hear it, Nyce. It's the first game and people wanna hear from the franchise player."

I wasn't in the mood to be nice to anyone. All I wanted was to get cleaned up and prepare to head out tomorrow. Since Reign didn't make it for the game, there was no reason for her to fly down. I was furious but had to compartmentalize to get my head back where it should be. Zane and I followed Coach into the designated room and made our way to the table as cameras flashed, and reporters yelled our names. Once we were settled, the questions started.

"Nyce, you had a rough start to the night, but you picked up there, right at the end. Do you think the score wouldn't have been so close if you showed up from the start?"

I looked over at Zane. This was the kind of silly questions that boiled my blood. "What do you think?"

The room went up in a laughing frenzy. I winked because I knew this guy. He was always on my case. He was the one that wrote a piece criticizing my game and questioning my pay. I was cool because he had the right to do it and it didn't seem personal, but now wasn't the time. A few more questions were asked which Zane and Coach took. A few moments later, I heard my name. I knew that voice and shook my head. I was not with the nonsense tonight.

"So, Cheta, we noticed your fiancée isn't here tonight. There's a rumor circulating about trouble in paradise. Looks like she's rekindling things with her ex back home," Simone asked.

"Repeat that?" I acted like I hadn't heard her question. The old me would have cursed, said some foul stuff, and stormed off. But it would be a cold day in hell if I gave these folks, especially her, something else to add to her sleazy commentary. Blood rushed to my brain and heat traveled up my spine. I had to get out of here.

"I said—"

"Next and final question," Coach said, cutting her off.

No one spoke. Instead, hushed voices floated through the room. I stood to leave. Once I was in the locker room, I forfeited a shower and grabbed my phone and bag. Tossing my bag over my shoulder, I headed out the backway to the parking garage. I heard some people call my name, but I ignored all of them and powered on my phone. Getting into my rental, I flung my bag to the passenger's seat, while my phone steadily buzzed in my hand.

I checked the barrage of notifications. I'd been tagged on

Instagram and Twitter with the same photo. The shot was a little blurred, but it was definitely a photo of another man's lips on my fiancée's. My phone rang and I immediately sent Reign to voicemail. My eyes narrowed, zoning in on the picture as I bit my bottom lip with the aim of drawing blood. I ignored a second call from Reign. The sting in my chest caused my hands to tighten around the steering wheel. I clenched my teeth, reading the captions.

"Trouble in Paradise?"

"Did Small Town Love Win in the End?"

"Good Guys Can Get the Girl."

Asa m: Babe, please answer the phone.

Amara: Don't say anything until we talk. I'll set up a Zoom for the AM

Marcus: Has Amara texted you yet?

In my fury, my mind went back to the day we negotiated this fake contract in Atlanta. Reign looked me in the eyes and pleaded with me not to make her look stupid. The joke was now on me. Blogs made up stuff every day, but pictures don't lie. I knew for sure they didn't photoshop this dude's lips on hers.

The way she kept calling me also let me know there was some truth to what I was seeing. If I spoke to her, I was bound to say something I couldn't take back. Disrespect was huge for me, and she'd violated in the worst way. It was best for me to power off my phone and that was exactly what I was about to do when a notification came through from the group chat with my cousins.

Nze: Don't do anything irrational. You know how the press is.

Jidenna: I agree. Cheta, *nwanyo*.

Ignoring them both, I powered off the device, started the engine, and sped out of the parking garage.

12

———

REIGN

"I been knew that man was the devil," Deja said.

I was irritated and felt off balance. Lifting my hands, I tugged at my hair. My frustration level was at an all-time high. I wasn't used to this kind of intrusion. For the past couple of months, the press had really let up and even if they had something bad to say, Cheta *and* I were the subject matter. Now I was the one being dragged all over these social media streets and I wished this nightmare would go away.

Never in my wildest dreams would I have imagined that any drama concerning our relationship would come from me. I loved Cheta and I knew for sure the feeling was mutual, but somewhere in the recesses of my mind, I did think he would mess up in some way first. After all, his reputation did take years to build.

I paced the length of my living room with my iPad in my hand. I studied the headline that appeared online a few hours ago. "Reign Davis: Worthy of an Award." It'd been a week since that stupid picture was put out into the world and the keyboard thugs weren't tired yet. In the first few days, Cheta gave me the silent treatment. I didn't know that would hurt as bad as it did. He had been my protector, my Che Bear—a nickname he

135

detested, but was fitting because with me he was all bark and no bite. He was the clingier one of both of us. The absence of that had me off balance. I missed my man.

"Martrell is the least of my problems right now," I responded to my sister who was on speaker phone.

"I agree. What's done is done. All we have to do now is find a way for you to get your man back," Ebonie said, popping a chip in her mouth.

I rolled my eyes at her. This was one of the things I liked and also couldn't stand about her—nothing seemed to bother her. I was having a life crisis and she was balanced on my couch with her feet under her like we were talking about the latest TV show.

"My in-law still has you in the doghouse?" Deja cackled.

"You know men and their ego. Besides, he told you not to go so many times. Give him time to sulk."

The days after the news broke, Cheta wouldn't answer my calls, so I called Martrell, desperate for him to feel my wrath. The way he answered the phone told me that either he knew there was a camera close by or he'd called one there himself.

When Cheta wanted to be, he could be so cold and unwelcoming, which was his current demeanor. When we finally met up, the disdain in his eyes was gut wrenching.

"Baby, I promise you they got it all wrong. I didn't kiss him."

"Oh, let me guess, he kissed you?"

"Yes!" I sighed. "You have to believe me? After we signed the papers, the Uber I ordered to get me to the airport cancelled. I ordered another one, but they were too far out, so he offered to drive me." I raised my shoulders. "I didn't think anything of it. All that was on my mind was getting to you."

I had left out the part about how entering the car with him in retrospect was a horrible idea. No matter how harsh Martrell's messages had been to me about wanting nothing to do with me since I wanted to ruin my life, the whole afternoon, he sent subliminal messages about how good we could still be together.

He parked at the drop-off lane, helped me get my hand luggage out of the trunk and that was where it happened. I turned my face to thank him and the next thing I knew, his lips were on mine with a hand wrapped around my waist. It was so sudden and fast that it knocked me off kilter. I pushed him away with all the force I had when I regained my senses, but then it was too late.

"Well, that didn't happen either now, did it?" Cheta seethed.

We were in his living room, and an ugly feeling of unease threatened to consume me. We weren't living together or anything, but I considered his house my home away from home. Both of us, being private, spent a lot of time indoors. As I stood there, the awkward unwelcome feeling was really sending me. He threw the television remote on the couch and stood.

"You have me out here looking like a clown. I told you so many times I didn't trust him."

"I know you're upset, but aren't you kinda blowing this out of proportion? You know I wasn't being sneaky."

He turned toward me, arched his brow, and inclined his head. "Out of proportion? Okay. You got it..."

He went to move, and I grabbed his hand. "Babe, wait! I didn't mean it that way, but what happened to all that talk about not caring what people say? You know I'm telling the truth."

"The difference is I freaking love you!" He lifted the drink he had been nursing to his lips and took a sip. "They can carry on about me all day long, but you gave them the leeway to play in my face like I'm a punk. I'm winning games out here and all they wanna ask me is about my fiancée cheating on me."

Dropping the drink on the mantel, he pulled on his beard. "Not to talk of jeopardizing your name and business. I asked several times to go with you. I asked to let someone else go with you, but no. You were on your independent woman crap. You denied me the ability to protect you...to protect us. I know men like that. He ain't blind. He reads the blogs. He knows how well you're doing, sees us on social media, so this was a chance for him to get his sorry resource management business some clout."

I raised my hands, tired of being berated like a child. I understood it. If I had been hounded with a picture of him kissing another woman, I'd be livid. But what was done was done.

"Okay! I promise I get it, but I can't change it now. Amara sent out a statement on our behalf. Can we just move on?"

He grunted, but didn't say anything. I moved closer to him and wrapped my arms around his waist. Unlike earlier, he didn't recoil from my touch. Instead, he draped an arm around my shoulder and kissed my temple. A breath I was unaware I was holding escaped my nostrils, taking with it a weight I'd been saddled with for some time. I was about to say something when we were interrupted by his chef announcing dinner. I hadn't planned on staying, but I wasn't ready for another argument. I allowed him to lead me to the dining room, and we sat down to eat. The initial conversation was strained, but was void of the animosity and tension of earlier. At the end of the evening, we'd seemed to reach a truce and he was back on the road.

That was some days ago and I had been the only one initiating our communication since then. Glancing at my device, I perused the headline that came out earlier. It was the reason me, my sister and Ebonie were currently assembled.

The pictures both Cheta and I had posted days earlier had all kinds of vitriol thrown at us. Folks claimed we were putting up a front. This article *The Shade Space* and *Tatafo Tales* posted about me being worthy of an award—accomplishing the feat of humbling "The Nyce" seemed to be the theory the public was going with. I called Cheta and had been sent straight to voice-mail, so I called my girls. The pattern of him blocking me out when a headline that he'd obviously seen and didn't like was getting old. And I was sick of it.

"Rei?"

Deja's voice brought me outta my head.

"Yeah?"

"The man might be busy. Today is game day. Cut him some slack."

"I know my man. This ain't the first time we've been through game day—"

"But these are the conference finals. He's your man and very well might be different, but at the end of the day, he's still a man. He needs to compartmentalize so he can do his job," Ebonie said.

Deja concurred and I thought about what they were saying. I agreed with them to an extent, but I knew Cheta and his "I don't get mad I get even," had me hella paranoid. But I also knew that without trust, we were as good as over. I needed to talk to him after tonight's game. We had to get back on the same page, or I needed to start seeing things for what they really were and what my life would look like without Cheta in it. The vibe of our conversation would determine how quickly that decision needed to be made.

I pressed send on the last email for the night and set my laptop to the side. I picked up my tea and took a sip of the now cool beverage. Pushing out a loud sigh, I glanced at my phone. For several hours, I had been waiting for it to ring. The game had been over for an hour. Pre all this drama, any time I couldn't attend a game, I would get a call in the first twenty minutes after. It was now one hour and two missed calls later and this man hadn't called me yet. He was really losing his mind and I was the right one to help him find it.

To keep myself from calling him again, I had been responding to and crafting emails I had neglected when I left work earlier. Before Ebonie left, I promised I wouldn't jump to any conclusions. But this was ridiculous, especially since they won the game. Allowing my head to rest on the back of the sofa, I tried to still my rising temper by taking in deep breaths. By the third exhale, my phone vibrated next to me. Peeking at the device, the caller caused my eyes to roll and my heart to skip a beat at the same time.

"Hello?"

"Hey, wassup?"

My brows furrowed and I removed the phone from my ear. *Nah, this can't be Cheta giving me this dry greeting, knowing he's in the wrong.*

"Excuse you?"

"Rei, I'm about to get on the elevator—"

"You okay?"

"I'm straight. You need anything or can I call—"

"You know what? Forget it." Before he could respond, I disconnected the call. *Nah, this is not even about to happen this way.*

I tossed the phone on the chair and it started ringing again. Ignoring it, I picked up my mug and empty snack plate and headed for the kitchen. My chest burned with rage. "Sweet Love" by Anita Baker, my ringtone for him, continued to play in a loop as the ringing stopped and continued as I left the phone unanswered.

I washed up my mug and dish then wiped down the counters. If he wanted to be childish, I could be too. Hanging the kitchen towel on the oven handle, I switched off the lights and walked back into the living room. I picked up my phone and read the text Cheta sent in all caps.

ANSWER THE FREAKING PHONE

I rolled my eyes and picked up my laptop when the phone rang again. "What?"

"Don't ever hang up when I'm still speaking again. We've never done that, and we're not about to start," he seethed.

"I didn't know we were still doing anything."

"What does that mean? We hit a rough patch, but you're not going anywhere, and neither am I. We work through stuff, but without the disrespect."

"I'm sorry. But you're treating me like a contract and I'm tired of it." I plopped back down on the sofa.

"You gotta give me time, Rei. That I'm not feeling you, doesn't mean I don't love you."

"But I want you to feel meeeee…I said I'm sorry," I whined. I knew I sounded terrible, but I'd do anything at this point to be back on his good side.

Cheta chuckled. "You're just as spoiled as can be…"

"It's your fault and you can't take it back." I smiled.

"I'm not trying to take it back. I'm processing, that's all. You don't know what it feels like to be ridiculed publicly because of another person's actions. Especially someone you can't disassociate yourself from because they're a part of you."

My heart fluttered, hearing his confession. I closed my eyes, wishing I could go back in time and heed his advice when it came to Martrell. In that moment, I decided to tell him a story I hadn't told a soul. "Baby, I can't say I know what the last part feels like, but I definitely know what it means to be ridiculed publicly."

"What are you talking about?"

I picked up my laptop and headed up the stairs. "Where are you?"

"I just got in my room. You had me waiting by the elevator for you to pick up the phone. I'mma put you on speaker so I can heat up my food."

I felt him about to enter another tirade, so I ignored him and continued. "There's a reason why my parents are hard on me. And before you start, I know they can be disrespectful with it, but hear me out. So, remember how I told you I suffered from real bad acne, and I lived in the shadow of my sister…"

"Yeah."

"I struggled with confidence and my self-esteem for so long. Well, when I was in my senior year in high school, there was this new transfer. Man, he was so handsome. It wa—"

"Aye! Get to the story…"

I laughed at him. "Anyway, we struck up a friendship. Suddenly, girls who looked down on me or always made snide remarks about me, now wanted to be my friend. How foolish of me to think it was about me and not because they thought I had some special clout with Dwayne. That was his name…Anyway, one day they invited me out driving. I was so naïve—"

"Aye, if you use one more negative adjective to describe yourself, we're about to have a problem."

"Can you let me tell the story?"

"I ain't stop you, but you heard what I said."

"At first, we went to the mall. I swore I saw them shoplift some things, but then they talked to some guy in the store, and we passed without any further question. I bought my own stuff, but with their connections I had a huge discount, so I didn't dwell on it. All through that day, I wasn't aware Claire was mixing alcohol in her soda. When we—"

"Claire? I already know it's some spoiled Caucasian chick…" He smacked in my ear.

"Can you stop smacking in my ear?"

"Girl, I'm hungry and your story taking too long. By the way, I haven't heard you tell your man congrats for the day's win."

I rolled my eyes like he could see me. "If you weren't so busy dodging my calls, that was the first thing I wanted to tell you."

"Yeah, whatever."

"Congrats baby. I'm so proud of you. I knew you were gonna win. Can I continue now?"

"Go ahead…"

"Anyway, the five of us got back on the road. She said there was a party she was invited to. She wasn't going to stay, but had to drop off a gift. On our way, Claire lost control of the car and we ran into one of those warehouse storage facilities. You know those flimsy ones with the zinc roof. But for some sprained or broken bones, we were okay.

"However, the owner of the warehouse had damaged equipment and we spilled some oil. Long story short, the man pressed charges. Damage to property. For the equipment and the oil spillage. The judge showed no mercy. My parents were livid that I had brought shame to their name. Hospital bills for my broken arm and my cost for the damages all came out of their pockets. I was given six months in juvenile detention. Although I only served four, by the time I got out, I had lost my scholarship. There was some requirement I had to fulfill in person, and I didn't make it.

"Through the shame, and them having to dig out of their savings to send me to school, my parents never forgave me. They say they have, but all the things I've done to pursue my dreams, they've never agreed with. So, I know what it is like to be publicly humiliated, but I love you and I'm sorry."

I sighed; a load finally lifted off my chest telling him that story. I hated keeping it from him because we'd shared a lot of our traumas, insecurities, and fears, but I'd always held that part of me back. I scratched the back of my ear as the silence between us lingered.

Ba—"

"You mean my baby is an ex-con? How come we didn't see this when we did the background check on you?" He cackled.

"Shut up. I'm not an ex con and you did a background check on me?" I already knew they must have.

"Of course, do you know how much I'm worth? I ain't about to be tied to you and you got a criminal history." He paused. "I'mma need to fire Marcus because you do have a criminal history. How did he miss this?"

"Cheta, will you be serious!" He was annoying me with his jokes. He always kept me on my toes because I never knew what he was coming with. "I can't stand you, and my records are sealed …"

"Oh baby, you mad?"

I remained silent.

"A'ight, cool you know what it feels like. But I don't care about that. Have you met my woman? She turned all that mess around. She's ambitious, passionate, hardworking, God fearing, kind, not to talk of how fine she is. She spoiled, but that's on me and I'm okay with that."

A tear rolled down my cheek. I was about to respond when I heard a loud thud through the phone. "Babe, what's that?"

"I'on…what the… baby, I gotta call you back."

"Cheta, what's going on?"

"Rei, I'll call you back. I promise."

I wanted to insist he tell me what was going on, but then I was met with a dial tone. There went my good night's rest because I wouldn't be settled until he did call me back. It was a good thing tomorrow was Saturday.

13

—————

CHETA

*S*hock restarted my brain, jolting me to my feet. I turned, my brows furrowed, and my mouth fell open as I struggled to comprehend the sight before me. Laid out on the floor was someone I hadn't been in the same room with for years. My gaze darted to the door of my suite. I quickly replayed my actions of the last hour or so. I had my takeout in one hand, my phone to my ear and my gym bag across my chest when I made it in. But I was for certain there wasn't anyone behind me and I heard the click of the automatic lock. I couldn't have been so engrossed in my conversation with Reign that I missed a whole human being behind me.

"Finley? What the hell?"

I watched the woman I once had deep feelings for, scramble to rise from the floor. My eyes darted to my phone. Reign and I were already on shaky ground. I wasn't trying to have her misread whatever this was.

"Does Vance know you're here? Matter of fact, why are you here?"

She smoothed down her blouse. "Hey Che…I was wondering if we could talk."

She moved toward me, and I stepped back. What was it with all these reunion sessions people suddenly wanted to have? First it was Chantel, Arinze's ex, then Reign's and now Finley.

"That's obvious, but I don't understand why. Didn't I have my girl on the phone when I told you some months ago to let me be?"

"Yeah, but I thought that..." she shrugged. "Well, since you and Rainbow are—"

I thumbed my nose. "We're not even about to play that game. You know her name." It would be over my dead body that anyone disrespected my woman in front of me. Behind me, was a risk I wasn't sure they wanted to take either. I leaned against the bar and folded my arms across my chest. I was treading on shaky ground letting her continue to be in my room.

She raised both her hands. "Sorry. It's just that I wanted to know why?"

"Why what?"

"Why did you change for her? Why her? She's not even..."

"Didn't I just tell you to watch it?"

Finley thought that her family name and obvious clout could get her anything. That was one thing that was always a bone of contention in our relationship. She thought she could push me around because of who her father was – Lt. Col. Dalton, a former ambassador. It wasn't until she got a glimpse of my "African family," as she put it, that she understood that I wasn't a ball player that needed an NBA deal to bring my family out of poverty. That reality check came when the whole family assembled in the U.K for my cousin, FiFi's graduation. I knocked nobody's hustle, but I was a different breed. I came from money.

She ran her hand over her fresh weave and paced back and forth. "I mean we dated for four years. No time did you even act like you wanted to be married. In fact, you told me all the time that you didn't." She let out a heavy breath. "I love you and you loved me, so why couldn't I be your fiancée. Why her?"

I snickered. "I see you haven't changed. You have a funny way of rewriting history. I was honest with you. Not once did I cheat on you, but I didn't want to get married. It—"

"So, you just decided to marry her? Where did she even come from?"

I turned because this had to be a prank. "Tell me when the cameraman will jump out." I frowned. "Have you forgotten the part where I had an accident, and you couldn't wait around? Instead, you hopped on my so-called best friend. Have you forgotten how I pleaded with you that my prognosis was good.? For you not to leave me?" I hit my chest and stood straight.

Now she had me hot. I hit my chest again. "I'm responsible for my actions, but you're the reason I acted like I didn't have any sense all those years. Making the press drag me through the mud. You froze my heart and now I have a woman who I need to breathe. One who makes me want to be better. One who doesn't see me as a dollar sign or is with me because of what I do. But is with me because of who I am. Simply Cheta Kalu. And why her? She's confident, hardworking, kind, compassionate but also no nonsense. She's also a boss in her own right. You see my skin…" I pointed to my cheek. "That's her stuff. I can hook you up if you want. But what we're not about to do is pretend that you're inno-cent or I treated you bad."

"But Che—"

I started toward the door. "Nah, we're done. I don't even wanna know how you got in here. Groupies do it all the time and I put nothing past you. I—"

She narrowed her eyes at me. In a flash, the puppy eyes she sported turned into fiery ones. "For real? You're calling me a groupie now?"

"That ain't what I said, but come on, you gotta go." I knew I was already setting myself up by even entertaining this conversa-tion. I kept my eyes on her as she picked up her purse and headed to the door. Her searching eyes roamed my face, but I remain deadpanned, focusing on the door I had open. She came to a halt in front of me, but instead of engaging her, I inclined my head toward the door, and she strolled out. Locking it behind her, I let out a deep breath I didn't know I was holding. Sauntering over to the curtains, I checked each one of them, ensuring there were no more unwanted guests lurking behind them. Satisfied there weren't, I cleaned up my mess, picked up my gym bag and headed to the room for a shower. All the while trying to figure out exactly what to tell Reign.

~

The blare of the wakeup call I'd requested pierced my eardrums, causing me to wince in pain. I felt for the phone on the nightstand. I answered the call, grunted my thanks and hung up. With my eyes still closed, I massaged my temples to ease my discomfort. Headaches for me were always hard to get rid of and I should've known I'd get one from hanging out after a game.

I'd wanted to fly home to celebrate our Eastern conference title win with my woman. Those plans were nixed when Reign had to take an impromptu trip to Spain earlier in the day. Her sister, Deja, had an emergency appendectomy and she wanted to help her out. Feeling bad about not being here with me, she encouraged me to hang out with the team. Since the last time we talked, I'd been back in Atlanta for a home game. A game I thought would be the end of the series, but Boston had managed to put us in a tie. Hence, I was back out in Boston for the final game.

Groaning, I pulled myself to a sitting position. Turning on the lamp, I adjusted to the light and searched for my phone. I knew it should be a few minutes after seven. The plan was for the team to meet for breakfast and be ready to board the plane by nine a.m. for takeoff back to Atlanta. I reached under the pillow, and frowned as I studied the device. I had several social media notifications which really didn't bother me. The Atlanta Harriers were now headed for the NBA finals, so folks had been tagging me since last night.

My heart thumped though at the number of repeated missed calls I had from my publicist, agent, cousins, and my dad. I went to my text icon. The group chat with Nze and Jidenna, the thread for my publicist and agent all had several unread messages. The one I clicked on was the one from an unknown number. It was in all caps.

HOW COULD YOU DO HER LIKE THIS? I'M SO DISAP-POINTED. I HATE YOU FOR EVERY TEAR MY SISTER SHED TONIGHT. DEJA.

My heart thumped against my chest as confusion washed over me. Hopping out of bed, I dialed Reign. My call when straight to voicemail, indicating I had been blocked. Opening Instagram, I made my way to the bathroom. The first tag I clicked on caused me to stumble against the sink. I blinked a few times to clear the fog I must have been in as I read the title to an article.

"Reign Davis: From Ex Con to Skincare Guru to NBA Fiancée."

In a panic, I browsed through the article written by Simone Baxter. It had a detailed version of the story Reign gave me last week about her troubles in her senior year of High School. The article talked about how her parents, leaders in the church, had a daughter who was once out of control. It had details like Reign's school, the number of girls that had been charged with her, the name of the business that the girls destroyed. There were no details of their time in juvenile detention because as Reign explained to me, the records had been sealed.

It did talk about her rise through the years, but then went on to insinuate that the reason we got engaged was because Reign needed help appearing respectable in time for her deal with Coleman. Closing out the piece, Simone asked her readers whether they thought Reign was truly in love with me, or her ex she was spotted kissing some weeks ago.

My chest tightened as I went down the list of tags I had from the most popular blogs.

"The Reckless Past of Cheta Kalu's Fiancée."

"The Nyce and His Not So Nice Fiancée."

"All That Glitters Really Isn't Gold."

"Cheta And Reign: A Match Made in Messy Heaven."

Each reiteration of the story was the same with a slightly different twist. What they all blaringly had in common was the slander on Reign and questions about the validity of our relationship.

Despite the air-conditioned room, sweat gathered on my forehead. Deja's text now made sense. They thought I was the one that leaked the information. I dialed Reign again and got the same result. Then I dialed Deja. After ringing for a few seconds, the call went to voicemail.

I called my lawyer, Clifton. He was out of the country, but with what I paid him, I needed him to drop every other thing for this. Getting no response, I left a voicemail. Dropping the phone on the counter, I bowed my head and took a breath. I called on Jesus for help as my world spun around me. The phone buzzed on the counter causing my eyes to spring open. My hope deflated when I noticed Jidenna was the one calling me. He couldn't help me right now and I had no answers for him, so I sent his call to voicemail. Then I shot him a quick text of a promise to call him back. Then my phone started ringing again. This time it was Amara.

"Cheta—"

"Amara, before you start...please get with Clifton. I need you guys to do any and everything—now—to get those articles taken down and cease and desists sent out. I don't care how much it costs. Immediately, *biko*. My wife is being dragged through the mud for a teenage mistake." I took a breath. Hearing nothing from the other side, I croaked out, "Amara?"

"Is it true?" she asked.

"Yes, but not the way it's being spun."

"Who leaked it?"

"I don't know, but those are all things that can be addressed later. Right now, I want those articles down and no other variation of it going up."

"Love looks good on you. I ne—"

"Amara!"

"All right, sit tight let me do my job."

"Nah, I can't do that, I'm heading to Spain—"

"Wait. What? Why?"

"Because that's where Reign is, and I need to talk to her." I turned on the faucet and picked up my toothbrush.

"Cheta, you can't do that. Hold on."

Frowning at the phone, I asked why. Amara went on to remind me that the finals started in three days and as the franchise player for the Harriers, I had obligations to fulfill before then. She warned against me risking it and getting stuck in Spain. I got her point, but that was what private planes were for. I needed a face to face with Reign. My sanity depended on it.

"I'm done talking about it."

I picked up a bottle of water and strolled to the treadmill in the middle of my home gym. I could feel my cousins' shocked eyes on me, but I was no longer in the mood to talk about what they were on. I had a life before Reign, and I was determined to have one after her. Anger bubbled in my stomach at the events of the past week, but I had a championship to win. And I wasn't going to let any woman throw me off my square. Even one that I loved. She'd done that in game one and some of game two. What

I'd wanted to be a 2-0 lead was now a draw and I had to get my head back where it belonged.

The championship.

Tomorrow night, we played game three here at home and that was my sole focus. This intervention my cousins thought they were having wasn't needed.

"C, you know you can fool everyone but us. This thing is bothering you, so why not try again?" Arinze asked.

I cut my eyes at him, lifting weights on the bench. His in-love behind was getting on my nerves and I was about to kick both of them out of my house.

"I see where you're coming from. It's been a week since the news broke. You risked being fined by going to Spain, only for her to turn you away—"

"Nah, let's get it correct, she knew what was on the line for me and she refused to see me. Even talk to me. How do you claim to love someone and won't even give them the benefit of the doubt?" I felt a headache coming on. This was the reason I was done talking about this.

Jidenna paused the elliptical he was on. "But, in all fairness, look at it from her point of view. You're the only one she told that story to. Her records are sealed. No one could have gotten—"

"If she really thinks I can hurt her like that, then she shouldn't be with me. So, I'm going to do her a favor and remove myself from the situation." I shrugged. "Her or her sister already told someone we were no longer engaged anyway."

"What about the contract?" Arinze asked.

"We ended it when we got back from *Naija*. I told Amara to tear it up. I mean we were building something real. I didn't want that hanging over us. She didn't take off that fake ring because we didn't wanna give the press any other thing to talk about."

"Good call," Jidenna said.

"And the "you are not engaged" thing that was probably said in anger," Nze said.

I got off the treadmill. "*Ngwa*...both of you need to get out. I got moves to make."

They both shared a look and chuckled, but I wasn't going to take the bait. I really did have moves to make. Zane, my teammate, was having a birthday dinner for his mother, and I'd promised to drop by if I could. I'd planned on sending a gift to her instead, but now I needed a distraction and my nosy cousins out of my hair.

"Cuz, we get it. You gotta concentrate on the game. But don't let this be another reason you start your "I don't trust women" campaign." Jidenna picked up a clean towel to wipe his face.

"But you see why though? Gave my heart to this one and she fumbled it."

Arinze picked up his key and headed up the stairs. "Stop being dramatic. Let the dust settle. Your team got all the articles down and stopped any others from going up. Odili took care of the *Naija* blogs. Chill out. She'll come around."

I grunted at the mention of my lawyer in Nigeria, Ekene Odili. He griped because he was vacationing with his family when I called to give him instructions. *Tatafo Tales* was my main target. Left to me, I wanted to shut their site down, but Ekene thought that would set a bad precedent.

"I'm chilling. Y'all the ones in here trying to have a Dr. Phil moment."

Granted I loved Reign, and my ego was bruised that she wouldn't even talk to me. But after the countless attempts, I was done. If there was the possibility of us having any future, she was gonna have to make the first step. She needed to hurry up though. There was a huge possibility that by the time she was ready, I would no longer be willing to give us a try. In the event she never became ready, I was gonna have to be okay with that too.

14

REIGN

"Okay, you need to get up."

My sister rolled her eyes and sucked her teeth as she picked up the snack wrappers on my bed. The room I had been occupying for the last week was a little untidy, but it wasn't enough to warrant her present hostility. I groaned as she opened the blinds and the sun rays hit my eyes. Tenting them with my hand, I pulled myself against the headboard.

"It's three in the afternoon and you're here sleeping like you don't have a whole business to run."

"Well, excuse me for coming to take care of my sister."

Deja scoffed. "I let it slip that I had an infection after surgery, and you hopped on a plane to help me." She clasped her hands together. "God knows I appreciated having my big sister here, but you're using this as an excuse to escape your life and I won't let you." She balled up some of my dirty clothes and threw them into the hamper. "I've never known my sister to be a wimp and you're not about to start now."

"You—"

She raised her hand. "You're going to say I don't know how it feels. Thank God I don't, but I won't let you throw away all you have worked for, over a heartbreak."

I shook my head and pulled off the covers. Walking over to the drawers where I had my things, I searched for some clean pajamas to change into once I had a shower. "Stop being dramatic. Ebonie is there, I'm checking in. My business isn't dying, but am I allowed to feel?" My voice was an octave higher than I wanted it to be, but everyone acted as though I hadn't explained this to them a thousand times.

My parents were ridiculed, which made them turn their wrath on me. We'd been cordial since I was able to replenish their retirement fund from the Coleman deal. This reopened that wound. I had been called everything but a child of God.

Cheta always told me he didn't get mad, he got even. He was the only person that knew that story, so who else would have said anything? There was nothing he could say to me. This was probably revenge for me disgracing him with the whole Martrell fiasco.

"You do know that feelings are fickle? I'd let you sulk if you had heard your man out. But you didn't. I hated him right along with you when I hadn't seen his actions. But sis, that man has moved mountains to get all the articles down and flew here himself. I mean at this point…" She shook her head. "I'm always gonna stand with you, ten toes down, but when the dust settles, you're going to regret the actions you're letting your feelings take the lead on."

Yeah, the articles were taken down, but if not for him, they wouldn't be public knowledge in the first place. I plopped down on the end of the bed.

"I hear you, but it hurts. I tried everything I knew to stay away from Cheta. Then I let my guard down and loved him more than I've loved any other man." I put my hand across my chest. "With him, I finally had belonging, and do you know what it did to my heart to read the story only him and my family knew about, splattered all over the internet?"

Deja sat next to me and pulled my head to lean on her shoulder. "Betrayal hurts. It's like a real stab wound. I get it, but here we're dealing with the perception of betrayal because you haven't given him an opportunity to talk to you. Even a blind person could see how good that man treated you. Why would he hurt you?"

I rested my elbows on my knees. That was the big question I had swirling in my head. Were all his actions smoke and mirrors? My heart literally ached, and I missed him. The first couple of days, I was enraged and then the tears wouldn't stop. After the clip I watched on Instagram last night, I was scared to pick up the phone. "I want to call him."

Deja stood. "Then do that."

I reached for my phone and played the clip for Deja. We watched as Cheta and one of his teammates came out of a restaurant and he was accosted by a reporter.

"Nyce, congratulations on your win tonight."

"Thank you. We're now in the lead and the only way we going is up." Cheta looked so good. He had on a cream and brown print polo over blue tapered jeans. He looked like he'd made a recent trip to the barbers and the diamond stud he occasionally wore in his ear was in tonight.

"Have you talked to Reign?"

"Who?"

"Your fiancée," the reporter clarified.

"I ain't know I had one of those." Cheta patted the man on his back and walked around him, headed to his car. Then the clip ended.

Deja turned to me and chuckled. "Is this why I had to come back from work and still meet you in bed at 3pm?"

"I'm happy he's winning, but how can he dismiss us like that?" I poked out my lips.

"First of all, with no ring on, we were in a public café when you proclaimed you're not engaged to him anymore. This world is small. Some silly person must have heard us and reported it to some blog. He probably saw it. Second, you know your man has no sense and doesn't address the press like that, so..." she shrugged. She stood and walked to the door. "I suggest you go get your man before he forgets even having a woman."

I could hear Deja's laughter from the hallway, but nothing was funny. My phone dinged again, and I opened my email. Rolling my eyes, I opened the fifth email I had gotten from this Simone Baxter character. She was the one that took credit for breaking the news about me being an ex-convict. All her emails read the same. She kept saying she had an opportunity for me, but I had ignored each one of them. There was nothing a woman who was bent on tearing me down could ever have to offer me.

It was as though she got high on Cheta's picture. Every critical article that had come out about his game during our relationship, she had written or was somehow quoted. He said he didn't sleep with her, and I believed him, but somehow, I was now doubting that. This obsession was ridiculous. As I had done all the others, I deleted the email.

Starting my shower, I absently watched the water run through my fingers as I waited for the right temperature. My mind ran down the events of the past week and the once familiar feeling of shame washed over me. Shame that I had allowed others to once again make me cower and hide. Deja was right. I wasn't a wimp. It was time for me to take back my power and the only way to do that was to start at the source.

"Ms. Davis, I'm so glad you decided to take me up on my offer."

Two days later, I was back in the United States and was standing in the *Atlanta Sports Today* offices. I turned to the voice of Simone Baxter. I'd gotten here a few minutes earlier and was told to wait in her office. During that time, my eyes roamed the walls of the space. From the pictures on the wall, she was quite accomplished in her own right. The woman had interviewed legends in the Atlanta sports arena. She'd also gotten some important awards from what I could tell. Why she decided to involve herself in sensationalism was beyond me. I knew she had an editor who had to approve her articles, but still.

She stretched her hand for a handshake, a gesture I ignored. I was not about to shake the hand of the woman that questioned my character without knowing me.

"And what offer might that be?" I asked.

She looked at her hand and put it on her hip as she rounded her desk. "Please sit."

"I'd rather stand. I won't be here long." I strolled to her award wall, letting a beat pass between us. Turning, I looked her square in her eyes. "The story you broke on me, who was your source?"

Simone smirked. "I can't tell you that. I mean what would I gain by revealing my sources? What I can give you is an opportunity to get your lick back."

My brows came together. Wasn't this supposed to be a reputable paper? Simone must have seen my befuddlement because she cleared her throat and quickly corrected herself.

"I mean your side of the story." She shrugged, then continued. "Of course, during the interview, you could also share some dirt on him. My offer is for you to do an exposé on Cheta. It's common knowledge that you guys are no longer together. From your almost year long relationship, surely you have something on him. Something that'll make him pay for…"

As Simone rambled on about all the reasons I would want to hurt Cheta, I saw her eyes bug and her body shake with excitement. How could someone be this excited about ruining another person?

"Stop." I rolled my eyes at her. "I have no idea what Cheta

could've done to deserve you being this pressed about ruining his image." Shaking my head, I picked up my purse that was on the chair. "It was a mistake coming here, but one thing I'll never do is give you dirt on him, even though he might have given you dirt on me."

Being in the same room with her had me double minded on the notion that Cheta would've told her anything.

"The details you shared in your story were things only he knew, apart from my family, of course. I still don't know how you got them, but hearing you now, I'm going to believe he didn't provide them. In fact, it no longer matters. That might be blind of me, but I now realize I've been focused on the wrong thing. All that man has shown me is love and consistency. For whatever he might've been in the past, he really is a great guy and has been so good to me. If in the end, he turns out not to be, that's my lesson. To learn from and eventually move on."

I turned to leave. "Have a good day, Ms. Baxter, and I suggest you find a new obsession. Cheta is no longer who you desperately want him to be."

Walking to the elevators, I calculated how I was going to grovel at Cheta's feet. Whatever I did would have to wait until after tonight's game. The Harriers were up 3-1 and he'd been playing great. Not being there hadn't stopped me from watching every game. There was a lot on the line for tonight's game which was being played here at home. A win would end the series and make them the NBA champions. It would be selfish of me to bring up our drama at such a crucial time. I was about to step into the elevator when I heard Simone call my name. Allowing the door to close, I waited for her to get closer.

"Look, despite what it looks like, I'm a sucker for romance," she said.

The way she'd been going after us, that was unbelievable. I deadpanned her, allowing her to continue her spiel.

"I did have an agenda getting you here, but I see you really love Cheta. I don't know if he'll be any better to you than he's been to the others, but I can tell you this…he wasn't my source."

Although I'd already made up my mind to believe him, relief washed over me. Then rage at what she admitted to next. Finely overheard my conversation with Cheta and told her about it. Rage took over my body. Without responding to her, I jabbed the down button with my finger. When the door opened, I got on and removed my phone from my purse. Locating the number I was looking for, I dialed and placed the phone to my ear. Seconds later, the door opened, letting me out in the lobby.

"Hey, Jas. It's me."

"Girl, I know who you are. Glad you finally decided to return my millionth call."

"Yeah, my bad. I'll explain later, but I need a favor."

"Where is he?" I asked Cheta's housekeeper the minute she opened the door. Walking past her, I made my way down the foyer to the first living room.

"Good morning Ms. Davis. Err…Mr. Kalu hasn't come down yet," she replied.

I returned her greeting, sighed, and apologized. I normally wasn't this rude, but this Sunday morning, Cheta had me acting out of character. It'd been exactly three days since the Harriers had won the championship and he still hadn't talked to me.

Oh, we had seen each other, but the man completely ignored me. When I called Jasmine that day, she told me that the whole family would be at the game. I told her of my plans to attend, but I didn't want to distract him. Agreeing with me, she got Arinze to change the plans of having the family sit courtside and have everyone in the family's skybox instead.

The awkwardness that ensued when I entered the skybox that evening was short-lived as everyone's attention quickly returned to rooting for Cheta. No one addressed the elephant in the room, and I assumed they were waiting to follow Cheta's lead once the game was over.

The game itself was nerve wracking, but at the end of the day, the Harriers became the new NBA champions, ending the series with a 4-1 victory. At the final buzzer, the family went down to the court to celebrate, but I decided to stay put. To my knowledge, Cheta wasn't aware I was there, and I didn't want to take the spotlight away from him. Jidenna quickly nixed that thought, dragging me along with them.

When Cheta noticed I was there, the fire in his eyes cut right through me, searing my heart. He didn't make a move or say anything to me, but quickly trained his expression to give off the happiness the night deserved. Luckily, reporters didn't care, or were over our drama because no major outlet said anything about me being there, only reporting on what was important. Their win. For that I was thankful, but now...

When the family went out to celebrate, Cheta continued to ignore my presence. From the corner of my eye, I saw when Arinze and Jidenna tried to talk to him, but he dismissed them both. I was grateful to Jasmine and Zola, because they kept me company. Since then, I'd been sending him messages which he clearly read, but didn't respond to.

Leaving the shop yesterday, I ran into Jasmine who wanted us to get together since the cousins were headed to Canada. Apparently, they were going to see Adaugo, Arinze's sister who got married last year and recently had her first child. The parade for the city's win was scheduled for next week and they were supposed to be back by then. The pity in her eyes when she realized I didn't know about the trip twisted my insides. I called Cheta, but as usual, my call went to voicemail.

Today, all that ended.

Leaving the living room, I headed for the stairs. Reaching his bedroom, I knocked once. Getting his permission to enter, I walked in. I spotted him in his sitting nook with his back to the door. I was sure he was journaling. That was another thing he did that I was sure his fans would be so surprised to hear.

"Esther, I—"

"What is it going to take?" I cut him off.

He turned, realizing it wasn't his housekeeper. The surprise in his eyes quickly morphed into irritation or anger—I couldn't tell which.

"What are you doing here?" Standing, he walked over to his nightstand and placed his journal on it.

"I want to know what's it gonna take?" I folded my hands across my chest.

"I have no idea what you're talking about. And it's too early for riddles."

"What is it going to take for you to talk to me?"

"Why should I?"

"Because we have unfinished business. I—"

"Last I heard, you finished it, so what is there to talk about?"

"Stop being facetious. Why didn't you tell me about Finley being in your room?"

Cheta pinned me with his gaze and then laughed. His prolonged cackle was beginning to annoy me.

"Oh, so let me guess, someone finally told you I didn't sell you out and now I deserve an audience?" He shook his head and made his way to his closet. "Man, get outta here with all that."

I blocked his path. He tried to walk around me, and I moved with him, blocking his path again. He stared down at me, but I didn't back down. I met and maintained our stare down. He leaned toward my ear.

"Reign, move out of my way, or I will remove you."

"You don't scare me, and I know you won't hurt me—"

"You do, huh? What happened to the monster that would sell your secrets to the highest bidder?"

"I never said that."

"You might as well."

"But why didn't you tell me about Finley? If you had—"

"Nah, we're not about to do that. I don't care what you thought. I should've been given the benefit of doubt. You women are funny. You talk about a guy showing you more in his actions than mere words. Where in our relationship, did I ever show you I could hurt you that way? I was gonna tell you about Finley, but we were already just getting ourselves back together after your dude's stunt—"

"He's not my dude…" I corrected.

Ignoring me, he continued, "But nothing happened. Before she could spew anymore of her nonsense, I kicked her outta my room. After that, I really didn't think about it…with the end of the semifinals. After the news broke and my panic settled, I remembered she was there. I tried to tell you, but you'd blocked me from having access to you. So, again, why are you here now?"

Hearing him say it, I really had no excuse for the way I acted. I could see the disappointment and hurt in his eyes and felt a tightening in my chest that I had caused those emotions. The silence was heavy and the tension thick as a few beats passed between us. He tried to move to the side, but I blocked him again.

"Reign, you gotta go. I have somewhere to be. You now know it wasn't me that leaked your secret. What else do you want?"

"For you to forgive me."

"You ain't apologized yet."

"I'm so sorry. I love you. Please forgive me. I'm sorry."

Cheta cupped my face with his palms. "I hear you, and I accept your apology. But I don't trust you, Rei. You let me walk through the best season of my life alone all because you didn't have faith in me…in us. You gotta know that whatever we had is done." He kissed my forehead and this time, was successful in getting past me.

Stunned by his response, I was stuck in place. Ebonie and Deja's warnings popped up in my head, but I couldn't have fathomed it actually happening. Hearing him say the words to me had my eyes stinging with tears. I'd mishandled the best thing in my life and now I had to live with the reality that I wasn't meant to have my happily ever after.

The irony of it all was that the contract we'd entered had my duties as his makeshift fiancée would've been expiring right about now. Maybe this was how it was meant to be. Whether it was true or my consolation story, I had to live with it. With that thought, I turned and walked away from possibly the last man I'd ever love.

Several hours later, back in my townhome, the melody of "The Goodness of God" by CeCe Winans played in the background as I tried desperately to get rid of the images in my head. Highlight reels of what Cheta and I shared played in my head in a loop. The places we'd visited, the times we'd fought, made up, prayed together and even argued over certain cultural differences.

A smile lifted the side of my mouth as I remembered him trying to teach me to eat fufu. Everything I'd let slip through my fingers pierced my heart with regret. Leaning back against my headboard, I chucked. After a few more spoons of Vanilla Strawberry ice cream in my mouth. I closed the container and put it on my nightstand.

After I had gotten back from Cheta's, I tried to distract myself from my misery by engaging in housework. With my house tidy, I took a shower, changed into some clean pjs and slipped back into bed. I knew Deja would kick my behind if she saw me, but it was only for today. Tomorrow I'd get back to business, but I was going to sit in my feelings without anyone making me feel guilty about it. Scooting under the covers, I rested my head on the pillow and shut my eyes, willing myself to sleep. It was going on midnight, and I had an early start in the morning. I had a nine a.m. meeting with some vendors, and some mixes to complete.

What felt like a few hours later, my phone buzzed. I groaned, rolling over to my side, I reached for the device. Once I had it in my hand, I squinted, trying to read the name on display.

Babe.

My eyes shot open, and I pulled myself up.

I'm not opposed to working on the damaged trust between us. If you agree, come to the parade with me...as a friend.

A sudden warmness enveloped my heart. It was a little after three a.m. That could only mean he was thinking of me as much as I was thinking of him. I couldn't wait to see him next week.

There was hope.

15

CHETA

hree months later...

"I want food."

I carried Reign on my back, chuckling at her whining. My baby had been through it today. I told her that a camel ride through the dessert and a hike up a portion of the Atlas Mountains wouldn't be an easy feat, but she thought it would be "fun." This, her acting like she didn't have any bone in her body as I carried her up the short path to our resort, was the result of her "fun."

"You sure you don't want any more fun?" I laughed. I jogged up the few stairs leading into the Grand Amour Spa & Resorts.

"Stop laughing at me and no." Her hand went tighter around my neck. "Stop jogging, my body hurts."

"That's it. When we get back home, I'm getting you a personal trainer. Ain't no way you can be hanging with me and a little hike is gonna take you out."

"Welcome back Mr. Kalu, Ms. Davis," Salma DuBois-Arazi

approached us with a smile. "I hope you enjoyed the day's excursion."

Reign grunted.

I and Ms. DuBois-Arazi shared a chuckle.

"Or at least tried to," Ms. DuBois-Arazi corrected.

"I've loved everything you've recommended to us so far, except that." Reign motioned for me to put her down.

"Well, I'm sure tonight's meal will more than make up for it. My brother is catering your experience himself," Ms. DuBois-Arazi said. Her eye caught another guest and she excused herself.

I wasn't disrespectful by a long shot, but I had eyes. Salma DuBois-Arazi was a vision to behold. She didn't have anything on my baby, but I now knew why Arinze's cousin, Qasim, was so pressed.

Taking Reign's hand, I escorted her through the lobby to her villa. "You gonna be okay?" "You want me to come run your bath?"

"No, I can manage. The quicker I get cleaned up, the quicker we can have our fancy dinner. I want food."

"Greedy. Not like you'll eat off your plate. You'll spend the evening eating off mine." I brushed my lips against hers. When I tried to deepen our lip tango, she pushed me back.

"Go."

I waited for her to enter and the lock to click before I turned and headed to the next villa which was mine.

I strolled in the door and my phone started to buzz. I reached in my pocket and as suspected, it was the group chat with my cousins. I shook my head at their impatient behinds. I told them to add Morocco to their world clock so they would know the time to text, but they couldn't obey instruction to save their lives. I ignored them and headed for the closet to pick out what I was wearing to dinner.

Several minutes later, hot water cascaded down my body as the last three months came to mind. When Reign left my home that day, I couldn't get her out of my mind no matter how I tried. It was never a matter of not loving her, but how she did me really stung. I was going to give it like a week and call her when I got back from Canada. In what capacity I wanted to deal with her again, I wasn't sure.

But leave it to my cousin, Ifunanya to call me at the right time. She listened as I told her about Reign's side of the story and where I stood on all of it. Her painting the hypothetical of Reign getting another man had me spiraling down into a different realm. Hence the text in the wee hours of the morning.

Reign was ready to give the "friends" thing a try and for a while, she was content with what I had to give. After a few weeks, I could tell that she was antsy about us getting back to where we used to be. She never said anything, but it was in her actions and attitude. Her desire came to a head when I was in New Orleans several weeks back.

I'd gone to a dinner with some brand execs that wanted me to be their spokesperson. I was there with my agent and a husband-and-wife team. Leave it to the press to take a picture at the time Marcus went to take a call and the woman's husband went to the bathroom. The blogs went crazy with all kinds of headlines and so did Reign.

She accused me of not wanting to put a label on us because I wanted to have my options open. Then accused me of not really forgiving her. My baby was hilarious, but I dared not laugh at her rage. I tried to calm her fear, but I mustn't have done a good job because either Deja or Ebonie must have told her it was a good idea to play with me.

From New Orleans, I had to go to NYC. It was there I received a picture of Reign out to dinner with some dude. That was the only time I appreciated the messy bloggers. After verifying it wasn't business, I sent her a text. Words I remembered to this day:

We're not together but you're mine. Don't play with me. Get rid of him.

She'd called me repeatedly, but I sent her to voicemail. The next day, I was in Atlanta at her doorstep. We hashed out our differences. And by that, I meant, she yelled, I was calm, then she became annoyed at my nonchalance, and yelled some more. I then roared until we came to an understanding. A new beginning —she was mine and I was hers. I grinned remembering that day. Turning off the shower, I stepped out. After brushing my teeth, I began getting ready for dinner.

~

"I hope you enjoyed your meal. For dessert, you'll be having meskouta," Omar DuBois Arazi said.

Reign listened attentively as he described a cake infused with lemon and frosted with a sweet lemon glaze. After he answered her question about substitutes to the recipe, he left.

When I told my boy, Niyi DaSilva, that I was planning to take my woman somewhere in Africa for a couple of days, he suggested Morocco. In three weeks, I'd be starting my final season with the NBA, and I wanted real alone time with Reign. We'd been back in a relationship for about seven weeks now and not to be a cliché, but our tests had made us stronger.

I didn't want to go to all the usual places like Cape Town, Zanzibar, or Seychelles. I wanted something romantic, but also a gem. He suggested Grand Amour Spa & Resorts in Tweede Kans Cove, Morocco. The pictures he showed me in his phone from when he came for his producers wedding didn't do the place justice. It was beautiful. The fact that it was owned by siblings reminded me of how close my family was. This was our last night here and if everything went according to plan, it would be the best night of my life.

I looked across the table and the brightness and joy in Reign's eyes made my heart beat a little faster. I loved everything about her. The white halter dress she wore at my request brought out the glow of her skin. Her ginger locs were up in a bun with two tresses hanging down at the sides. The diamond stud necklace and bracelet pair I'd given her for Valentine's Day shone bright in the low lights of the VIP area we were in.

About an hour later, Reign and I strolled hand in hand along the beach. My blazer was draped across her shoulders to shield her from the chill of the night. For extra protection, she was tucked under my arm. We didn't have to talk. That was another thing I loved about us; we didn't always have to say anything. No performance—just being.

"You know I love you right?" I asked.

She halted her steps and looked up at me. "Yes, and I love you, too." She studied me and I felt her in my soul. "What's wrong?"

"Nothing. I don't wanna lose this." I pointed between us.

"And we'll do the work to make sure we don't."

I palmed her face with both hands. "Reign Davis, who I am with you is someone I never imagined I could be. All I've done, all I've been through has brought me to this moment with you. The smile on your face is a daily need for me. You've become my best friend, my shoulder to lean on, and not to forget skincare consultant." I bent on one knee.

My girl was such a crybaby. Tears rolled down her cheeks.

"You're the love of my life. Marry me, please."

"Yes, yes, I'll marry you." She continued to whimper and wipe the tears from her face, nodding.

I reached into my pocket and retrieved the ring I had removed from its casing earlier. Taking her hand, I slid on the platinum Sankofa heart emerald ring. The emerald center stone was five carats and accented by white sapphires on each side. With all that green she loves, the minute I saw it, I knew it was for her. After she examined her new piece of jewelry, she pulled me down for a passionate kiss. Knowing I had something else to ask her, I broke our kiss.

"I got another question, baby."

"Yeah?"

"Will you marry me—"

"I already said yes."

I chuckled. "Now. Will you marry me now?"

She looked confused for a minute, but I was determined to leave Morocco a married man. We'd been engaged, fake or not for almost a year. That was done.

To convince her I continued. "You can have the biggest or smallest wedding you want. We'll do the whole Naija traditional thing you and Jas can't seem to stop talking about. But I need you to be my wife, now."

She shrugged. "Okay."

Giving her a quick kiss, I grabbed her hand an walked a few more feet where the officiant was waiting for us.

Her eyes flew open in shock. "Oh, you mean now, now." She looked from me to the officiant. "I guess you were confident I was going to say yes."

"You should know I always intend to get what I want. I told you, no slackers on my team."

After a few words, we said our vows and were pronounced man and wife.

"Come here, Mrs. Kalu." I used my index finger to motion for her.

Beaming, she took a step forward and I dipped my head to take the full lips I'd never tire of for the rest of my days.

THE END

GLOSSARY

Pidgin/Igbo Translations

The Kalus are from Enugu State located in the South Eastern part of Nigeria. They're of the Igbo ethnicity. Below are translations (done to the best of my ability) to the languages I used in the story. I have this in the order in which they appear.

I dey feel am, but anything else I no know: I'm feeling her but other than that I really don't know (Pidgin)

hapụ ya: Leave it (Igbo)

Mba: No (Igbo)

anụla m gị : I've heard you (Igbo)

Asa m: My beauty (Igbo)

O we ife ne me gi nisi: Is something wrong with your head or are you crazy? (Igbo)

Abeg: Please o (Pidgin)

How far?: How are you? (Pidgin)

Oga: Prefix that shows sign of respect. Like "sir" (Pidgin)

Nkwobi & Nsala: Native delicacies of the Igbo people

Ke kwanu: How are you? (Igbo)

E bia la: You've come (Igbo) In context, it means "you've started"

You dey vex?: Are you angry/upset? (Pidgin)

Nwanyo: Easy (Igbo)

Biko: Please (Igbo)

Ngwa: Quick (Igbo)

FINAL NOTE

Thank you for reading Cheta & Reign's story. Please consider leaving a review/rating on the platform you purchased the book. I greatly appreciate your honest feedback. They really go a long way. The number of reviews a book receives greatly improves its visibility.

If you liked this story, I trust you might like some of my other titles. But before we get to those, I'd love to stay connected. Never miss a sale, new release announcements, or freebies. You can ensure you're in the know by joining my mailing list.

Next up in the Kalu family is Jidenna Kalu. Preorder your copy today with your favorite online retailer.

ALSO BY UNOMA NWANKWOR

Stand Alone Books

An Unexpected Blessing

He Changed My Name

When You Let Go

Full Circle

The Ultimatum Series

The Christmas Ultimatum

The Final Ultimatum

Sons of Ishmael Series

A Scoop of Love

Anchored by Love

Mended with Love

Redeemed Through Love

Mixed Tidings

The Invisible Shackles Series

To Live Again,

To Breathe Again

The DuBois-Arazi Family Novels

A Promise Fulfilled

Destiny Fulfilled

The Billionaire Pact

Vegas Nights

Second Shot

Pretend Bae

Away To Africa

New Year's Kiss (Prequel)

Rent-A-Bae

His Makeshift Fiancée

*A Suitable Wife (**Available for preorder**)*

www.ingramcontent.com/pod-product-compliance
Lightning Source LLC
Chambersburg PA
CBHW021711190726
48289CB00008B/2476